MARKED FOR DEATH

In the gloom to the right of the wagon Clint could hear footsteps running away. He looked down at the ground and in the light of the quarter moon spotted Sally Raines. He knew she was dying.

Clint gently lifted her into his arms and then brought her over to the wagon. She turned her head towards him. The flickering light of the kerosene lamp showed the tears in her eyes. She said haltingly, "In my pocket . . . there's a note. Take it out."

"You'd better not try to talk. I'm going to get you into town," Clint replied.

"It's too late," Sally said. "My pocket . . . the note . . ."

Clint took the note from her pocket and read it several times.

I know who killed Helen. Come to Dante,
Colorado within two weeks and I will tell
you. Don't worry about finding me. I will
find you. . . .

Don't miss any of the lusty, hard-riding action in the Charter Western series, THE GUNSMITH

And coming next month:

THE GUNSMITH #63: TEXAS TRACKDOWN

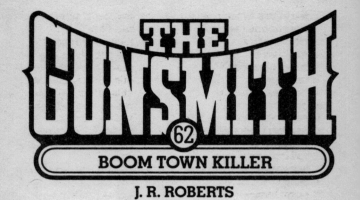

THE GUNSMITH

62

BOOM TOWN KILLER

J. R. ROBERTS

C

CHARTER BOOKS, NEW YORK

THE GUNSMITH #62: BOOM TOWN KILLER

A Charter Book/published by arrangement with
the author

PRINTING HISTORY
Charter edition/February 1987

ISBN: 0-441-30966-6

Charter Books are published by The Berkley Publishing Group,
200 Madison Avenue, New York, New York 10016.
PRINTED IN THE UNITED STATES OF AMERICA

ONE

Outside in the darkness of the western night a figure in black crept towards the wagon that was pulled off the stage road . . .

"Oh, Clint," Sally Raines sighed as she moved into the Gunsmith's embrace. "I've just been waiting two whole days for this."

The buxom red-haired young woman trembled as she pressed her body against Clint Adams and closed her eyes.

It was almost eleven o'clock in the evening, in northern Colorado, outside of a town called Dante. The fog had proved so heavy on this chilled September night that Clint had decided to pull off the road rather than risk damaging his rig or injuring his team or Duke.

Two days before he had come across Sally Raines, whose wagon had broken down, back on the stage road. She'd taken what belongings she could carry and accepted Clint's invitation of a ride with him to Dante, where she was supposed to meet a "lady friend." Clint had a strong suspicion about Sally Raines' occupation, but he was too much of a gentleman to say anything. If the woman wanted him to know, he figured she'd tell him. If not, that was okay, too.

"Oh, Clint," she moaned again, as they both eased down to the floor of the rig.

Her hand found his swelling penis. There could be no doubt what would happen next.

She stroked his cock while kissing his chest, running her tongue around his nipples. She worked her way down until her nose was right up against the swollen head of his cock, and then she began to run her tongue up and down its length, fondling his testicles at the same time.

Clint moaned when the woman finally took him into her mouth and began to work on him expertly. . . .

After a violent explosion of passion that left his legs weak, they switched position and now it was the Gunsmith's turn to use his tongue, running it over the woman's large, firm, breasts, sucking her nipples until they were as hard as cherry pits.

He licked her body avidly, as if trying to clean off the random sprinkling of freckles, and then he started to lick her inside, cupping the cheeks of her ass so he could lift her off the floor of the wagon while he lapped at her.

Then finally he was in her, and the wagon was bucking and rocking as they writhed against each other, trying to get as much as they could from each other because they were strangers, and who knew whether this was the only time they'd have together?

Each wanted to make the most of it.

• • •

Two miles away, in Dante, while Clint was taking his pleasure with the Raines woman, a somewhat comical little man in a checkered suit, red walrus mustache and black derby hat stepped up next to the six-foot-tall town sheriff and said, "This is exactly the kind of night the Ripper loves."

Sheriff Jacob Halsey looked down at the small man next to him. "Still peddling your trashy news stories, eh, Graves? Ripper!" The last was said in disgust.

Rupert Graves, a reporter for a most lurid London newspaper, smiled pleasantly at the sheriff.

"I would think you'd want to support my Ripper story, Sheriff. Otherwise the voters would hold you responsible for the four deaths in the past six months —and the election's only ninety days away. If they think the Ripper's really here in Dante, they may be more apt to forgive you. After all, not even Scotland Yard could catch him."

"The Ripper!" Halsey snapped. This time it was said angrily.

Halsey was a fleshy man dressed in a two-piece gabardine suit and a duster. He spat a stream of tobacco juice into the street.

"There've been murders in Dante, no doubt about that, but they haven't been the work of any Ripper."

"Oh? Then you've got a lead?" Graves asked. His voice reeked of skepticism.

"Let's just say I'm working on some things and leave it at that."

"Isn't that what you told me last week?"

"Believe it or not, Graves," the sheriff said impatiently, "I'm doing the best I can."

Graves flipped the cover of his little notebook closed with a flourish.

"Somehow I don't think the voters would find that reassuring."

With that he stuffed the notebook into the flat pocket of his checkered suit, doffed his derby and made his way down the foggy main street of Dante.

He hadn't been joshing Halsey about this being the kind of night the Ripper preferred. Graves had been born and raised in Boston. But ten years before he had gone to London and had covered the Ripper killings there, six gory slashings in the Whitechapel slum the previous year. Then the killings stopped amidst rumors that the Ripper, whoever he was, might have fled to America. Rupert Graves, ever intrepid—and stubborn—followed.

The first stop had been Texas, where a series of similar murders had taken place. From there he went to Nicaragua, where there had been a report of killings that had virtually matched the Ripper's.

Now, because a story had been seen in the *Chicago Tribune* about the brutal murders of two prostitutes in Dante, Colorado, Graves was here, investigating.

During the past two months two more prostitutes had been killed, slashed to death, with notes left behind. What had that last one said?

This is number four. Bloody dead is the whore. Count them up—there will be more.

The Ripper

Graves thought about all this as he started down Main street, unable to make out anything except the halo effect through the fog of Dante's glowing street lamps. He was smiling to himself about aggravating the sheriff when he heard the unmistakable sounds of footsteps on the boardwalks on either side of him.

He froze, terrified. Somehow he managed to find his voice.

"W-who is it?"

He could see nothing. The fog covered everything, swirling around like deep and murky ocean water. No matter how he squinted and narrowed his eyes, he couldn't see through it.

"W-who is it?" he called again. This time his voice hinted at the hysteria he was barely suppressing.

But of course there was no answer.

Just the footsteps moving closer to—*thunk-thunk-thunk*—against the boards. He stood there, frozen in terror. Helpless.

Later she put her head on his arm and they lay together.

"You're the sort of man I rarely meet, Clint Adams."

"You mean the kind who picks strange women up from the side of the road."

"And then makes them damned glad you did."

"I'll take that as a compliment."

"Damn right it's a compliment!"

They were silent for a time and then he said, "I hope you sleep a little better tonight."

The night before troubling dreams had caused her to get up and pace restlessly.

"So do I," she said earnestly.

She was asleep within five minutes, safe and sound within the circle of Clint Adams' arms.

TWO

Since his return to America Graves had become a great reader of dime novels. Such reading inspired him to believe that he was secretly capable of all sorts of acts of bravery—once he was put to the test.

Tonight—echoing, ominous footsteps—was just such a test and Rupert Graves flunked it miserably.

Through the currents of fog a silhouetted figure suddenly emerged and walked towards Graves.

All Graves could do was stand still and hope he didn't foul his pants.

"Hello?" Graves managed to call out weakly.

The advancing figure made no sound. There was just that looming shadow moving through the fog. Closer and closer . . .

"Hello?"

Then he heard a familiar laugh bark like a gunshot in the murk. Sheriff Halsey emerged from the mist and said, "You write real brave, Graves, but if you ever actually meet your Ripper—you'd be dead in seconds."

With that the sheriff walked on by, losing himself in the fog.

Graves could only stand there stunned and humiliated. The Sheriff had followed him for only one reason—to embarrass him.

And as much as Graves hated to admit it, the sheriff had done a damned good job of it.

All Graves could do was start gnawing once again on a plan to show the sheriff up for the incompetent he waš.

Distantly there was the ratcheting of a barn owl, not the sort of sound that would disturb most people used to sleeping out under the western sky.

Sally Raines, however, was different. She'd become a prostitute back in Omaha fourteen years earlier, when she was only twelve years old. She'd gone from there to the goldfields westward. In all those years she'd learned one thing above all: Sleep warily. You never knew who was going to creep into your room.

Sally had another reason to be frightened. She reached up and pulled her skirt down and felt in the pocket for the note. It burned there with its terrifying message.

In the goldfields Sally had learned to roll her own with a five cents bag of tobacco and cigarette papers. Afraid that the smoke might wake Clint, she made her way quietly to the front of the wagon so that she could sit outdoors and enjoy her smoke.

The night air was damp but it felt good, like taking a bath. She was happy tonight. Clint was the sort of man she'd often found herself dreaming of. He was tall and handsome, clean and hard but not so hard that he couldn't show a woman proper respect and tenderness.

She watched how the fog swirled around her, heard Duke nicker in the gloom. She struck a match and then inhaled deeply. After a few more drags on the cigarette Sally began to think about the note again.

I know who killed Helen. Come to Dante, Colorado within two weeks and I will tell you. Don't worry about finding me. I will find you.

A surge of anger went through her as she thought of Helen Tobin. The woman had been her best friend for ten years. They'd worked in more than ten different towns together and then Helen had been hacked and slashed to death.

She finished her cigarette, thinking of all the good times she'd had with Helen.

She didn't know who had written her the note, or why, but she was determined that once she got to Dante she was going to find out.

She flipped the cigarette into the rolling fog and made ready to back inside. But before she could even scream, the wagon creaked lightly as somebody leapt up on her from below.

There was the warm body smell of another human close to her, a glimpse of black clothing, and a gloved hand covering her mouth so she could make no sound as she was dragged to the ground.

Then there was the knife ripping deep into her chest, cutting left and right so that the damage was certain to be fatal.

She fought against her assailant but the shock made her struggles useless.

Distantly, she heard Clint coming awake.

The hand left her mouth and for the first time, she screamed—

THREE

Clint shook off sleep as he reached for his gun and raced to the front of the wagon. A quarter moon shone behind the fog.

Somewhere in the gloom to the right of the wagon Clint could hear footsteps running away.

For now he couldn't think of that, though. He looked down at the ground and spotted Sally Raines. The anger he always felt when confronted with the waste of death surged through him.

He lifted her gently into his arms and then brought her over to the wagon.

After laying her on the blanket where they had made love and slept he lit a kerosene lamp and started to look her over.

The assailant had used a knife and done so with expertise. A cleft had been ripped between Sally's beautiful breasts and her stomach was a tidepool of blood. Her blue eyes were wide with shock and pain.

He knew she was dying.

He wondered if she knew.

He knelt beside her and took her hand.

She turned her head slightly towards him and said, "Will you say a prayer, Clint, please?"

The Gunsmith flushed. He was not a religious man in any formal sense. He tried to remember the words of a Sunday School prayer from long ago.

"Lord, deliver us from our sins and make us all your children."

The flickering light of the kerosene lamp showed the tears in her eyes.

"Thanks, Clint." Then she said haltingly, "In my pocket there's a note. Take it out."

"You'd better not try to talk. I'm going to get you into town."

She looked at him frankly. Her breath was coming sharply.

"We both know better than that, Clint. A whore's life is not an easy one and I've seen enough death to know that mine is coming."

Clint tried to put a towel over the wound, hoping to slow the bleeding, but in moments the towel was soaked red . . .

She closed her eyes and he feared she was dead, then he noticed her lower lip twitch in pain.

"I'm going to get us into town," he said again, helplessly.

"It's too late, Clint," she said, "too late." Already her voice rattled with death. "In my pocket. The note."

She reached up and took his hand. At first the grip was like that of a small child, then briefly it became as strong as a man's. Her eyes never opened again.

Clint, too, had seen a lot of death in his time but he was still not accustomed to the violent death of a beautiful, gentle woman. Even if she was a prostitute, Sally Raines had dignity and humor and he'd come to like her a great deal in the short time since they'd met.

When he could bring himself to do it he reached into her pocket and pulled out the note she had been talking about. He read it several times, glancing over at the bloody corpse of Sally Raines.

He immediately had many questions.

Who was Helen? Who had written Sally the note? And most especially, why had the note been written to Sally?

He wondered if he should have gone after her assailant but he knew better. The killer would have been impossible to catch in the fog.

Catching the killer in the town of Dante, however, was entirely another matter.

Clint got the wagon ready to roll and by that time the fog had thinned out enough so that he could follow the road.

By the time he reached Dante the fog had burned off completely in the September sun and the town had come to life.

He immediately went in search of the undertaker.

FOUR

Dante was a town of 9,000 souls, a booming city by Western standards, and so Clint had to search a while to find the undertaker. He passed down a block of fine new buildings, a millinery, a druggist, an attorney, a hardware store and a bank in a long line to his right. The undertaker's was at the end of the block.

Clint went around back. He jumped down and went up to the door and knocked. A dandified man in a cutaway suit answered the door. The man had the eyes of a wild and hungry animal sighting food.

"Yes?"

"I have a body inside my wagon."

"A body?"

"Yeah, a body. That's your business, isn't it? You are the undertaker?"

The black animal eyes narrowed in anger but Clint did not give him a chance to speak.

"I need you to help me get her inside and see to it

that she gets a decent burial—the kind respectable folks get."

The man cleared his throat.

"That costs money."

From his pocket Clint produced some money. He counted out a respectable sum and handed it to the undertaker.

"I want to give you a little bit of a warning."

The man, preoccupied with counting the money in his hands, said, "Yeah, what?"

"I'm going to attend her services so I'm warning you in advance. I don't want any cutting corners. Do you understand?"

The undertaker nodded, his mind still on the money. Apparently he was not quite used to being paid this quickly.

Fancy carriages filled a few of the streets as Clint went in search of the sheriff's office. Gentrified men and women window-shopped and strolled in a leisurely fashion along the more modern streets of the town.

Clint turned right, into a rough section of town. Here the wagons were broad and crude, hauling dust, grime and metals from the surrounding mountains where mines were dug deep into rock. The people changed, too.

The men had a defeated air. Their dusty clothes said they were miners. The weaving way they walked said they were either taking the day off or had been fired. They went in and out of one saloon after another, for this block was a solid wall of saloons. The smell of beer was tangy on the air, and player pianos sounded comic so early in the morning. There was a lot of laughter but it was harsh, as if it lacked pleasure.

A miner stumbled out of a doorway and into

Clint. He was an old toothless geezer. He took a swing at Clint—as if Clint had been trying to get into a fight—and then looked shocked when Clint simply grabbed his wrists in a viselike grip and held him still.

"You look like one of Colonel Porter's men!" the drunken miner said. His breath could have melted a metal wall.

"Who's Colonel Porter?"

"Who's Colonel Porter?" The miner looked at him as if he were insane. "Why, the man who owns this town and the man who took all our pleasures away by givin' into the sheriff."

"I'm afraid you've lost me, old man."

"The whorehouses! The sheriff closed 'em all down. Now there's nothin' for us miners to do at night. That's why so many of us are quittin' our jobs and movin' on!"

"What's going to happen to the mines?"

"To hell with the mines! Nobody'll run 'em, not without some pleasure to be had, let me tell you."

The miner was joined by another old man who was just as drunk and ornery.

"Why you talkin' to this bastard?" the second man asked. "Get back in here and finish our pinochle game."

With that the new man jerked the other man from Clint's grip and back into the saloon. Clint could just imagine a card game between those two. They were too drunk to even hold the cards.

The sheriff's office could easily have been confused with a lawyer's fancy storefront office except for the word SHERIFF in gold script on a large window that looked in on several large rolltop desks. Men in three-piece suits and handlebar mustaches sat inside. On a trip to New York sometime back, looking for a dime novelist named Ned Buntline who had decided to profit by exaggerating tales about the Gunsmith, Clint had seen such lawmen, but rarely had he encountered this civilized breed of lawman out here.

He was about to walk up the three steps leading to the sheriff's office when he heard the unmistakable sound of the safety being let off a revolver.

"Hold it right there or you'll be meeting your Maker in less than three seconds."

FIVE

Five minutes later Clint was being led down a long corridor that smelled strongly of floor polish. The young deputy who had been behind him, a fleshy man whose high collar and walrus mustache gave him more the look of a barbershop quartet singer than a lawman, now stood next to a door and ushered Clint inside.

"This is the man Mr. Riley said killed that woman," the deputy announced.

The nameplate on the desk announced SHERIFF HALSEY. Halsey looked up from his paperwork. Though he was a big man, with a scar on his left cheek, his three-piece suit and big Cuban cigar gave him the image of a banker. The big Colt on his desk, however, quickly changed that impression. Obviously he kept it right near his hand in case he needed it.

"Sit down," he said.

Clint glanced over at the deputy. The man seemed

to glow in the presence of the sheriff.

"You heard the sheriff."

Clint sat down, wondering if there were any law-men in this town who *looked* like lawmen.

Halsey got right to business.

"You could be the man we're looking for."

"What man?"

"The man who killed four prostitutes here over the past six months, of course."

Clint's jaw muscles began to work.

"I don't take kindly to accusations, Sheriff," he said. He spoke evenly in an attempt to hold his temper. "Especially when killing women is concerned."

Halsey smiled and winked at the deputy.

"I seem to have upset our friend, here."

The deputy winked back.

"Sounds like you might have hurt his feelings. Ain't that a shame?"

"I bet I owe him an apology."

"Sure sounds like it."

"Well, I think I'll do that—just as soon as he confesses."

Now it was Clint's turn to smile.

"Maybe I can't prove that I didn't kill Sally Raines, the woman I brought in, but I can certainly prove that I didn't kill the others. I was in other parts of the country over the past six months."

"Doing what?"

"Mostly helping people keep their weapons in good working order."

"You're a gunsmith?"

Clint nodded.

"What's your name?"

"Clint Adams."

"Clint Ad—wait a minute," the man said, frowning. "Are you *the* Gunsmith?"

"That's what they call me."

"You can prove that?"

Clint took several forms of identification from his pocket and passed them to the sheriff. Halsey dragged on his big cigar as he looked them over. Instead of handing them back he held them out for his deputy to look at.

"You really are the Gunsmith, then."

Clint nodded.

"Looks like I really do owe you an apology," Halsey said. "You helped out a friend of mine one time when he got into trouble—a lawman named Reavers. A lynch mob was about to hang him *and* his prisoner but you stopped them. Every time Reavers and I get together he talks about you."

"I remember him. He's a good man."

"So I'm going to assume that you didn't kill— what did you say her name was?"

"Sally Raines."

"I'm going to assume you didn't kill this Sally Raines but I'd sure as hell appreciate it if you'd tell me what *did* happen."

Just as Clint was about to speak, the deputy, all flushed and excited, handed him back his identification with a hand that shook slightly.

"My name is Henry Leonard, sir, and I've heard about you all my life. I'd sure like to shake your hand."

Clint obliged the man, then filled the sheriff in on the details of Sally Raines' death.

"I feel responsible," Clint said.

"Doesn't sound like your fault."

"She's in my care, sort of—do you know what I mean?"

"I suppose you could think of it that way, but this killer of ours has been terribly successful with his murders. You're no more responsible for her death than I am for the four others."

"Could you tell me about him?"

"If you really want to know," the lawman said, "but it isn't pretty."

"It never is."

"Six months ago these killings started," Sheriff Halsey explained. "This one, in your wagon, sure sounds pretty much like all the others. Prostitutes hacked up the way animals are hacked on a killing floor."

"Tell me about the other killings."

"OK. How 'bout some coffee?"

"I'd appreciate it very much."

The deputy went out, and came back with the coffee in a fancy silver pot. He poured it into little flowered china cups.

"Why don't you fill me in about somebody called Colonel Porter, too?"

"I'll do my best to give you the whole picture, Mr. Adams," Halsey said.

"The name is Clint."

"Clint, then. My name's Burt. Colonel Porter was in the Union Army. Distinguished himself at the Battle of Fair Oaks. After the war the colonel came West and decided to take up mining. He had a great deal of luck right away and so he needed a lot of miners. However, the colonel is not like most mine owners. He knows from his days in the Army that you get the best men and the best work from laborers when you treat them with respect. So from the start the colonel paid the highest wages, gave his men the most modern equipment and instituted the strictest safety policies.

"Eventually, the first work force came here and formed a town, one so prosperous that merchants soon followed, and then craftsmen. Dante became a small metropolis in the middle of a range of mountains. If you've looked around I'm sure you saw that."

Clint nodded, remembering the new buildings and fancy carriages in the better part of town.

"Well, as much as he was civic-minded, the colonel has always been practical. He knew that the unmarried miners, who comprise the majority of the work force, needed places to spend their nights. So while Porter took care to make Dante into a model town he also saw to it that one end of the town had the sort of things unmarried miners wanted—saloons and whorehouses.

"The respectable people in town fought him, of course, especially as more and more middle class people moved in. But the colonel was adamant. He took care that the whores did not bother respectable people and I made sure that my men kept a tight rein on that end of town. Violence there was minimal, and respectable men mostly stayed away, except for the occasional straying husband.

"It was an uneasy truce at best but everyone seemed able to live with it until the killings started."

"You said six months ago."

The sheriff nodded, and tapped a chunk of ash from his cigar.

"The first victim was a sixteen-year-old prostitute," Halsey said sadly. "She was gutted, as they would all be. Now we've had four killings and the killer has left a note behind every time."

"What kind of note?"

"A rhyme of some kind, having to do with the victim being a prostitute. We've attracted a lot of attention because of it. Reporters from big Eastern newspapers are in and out of here, and we've even got some fellow all the way from England who thinks that our 'Ripper' resembles a Ripper they had there some time ago.

"Anyway, with the last killing, the so-called up-standing citizens got together and laid down the law to both me and the Colonel. They told me that they were running their own candidate for sheriff in the next election—a former U.S. Marshal named Smythe—and they told the Colonel that they would establish a union if he didn't close down all the whorehouses. They've got a Citizens Committee led by a parson called Robeson and they're just as demanding as any lynch mob I've ever faced. They don't believe in compromise and they believe exactly what they want to believe—and nothing else.

"As for me, I've pretty much gotten used to the idea that I won't be reelected. And as for the colonel, he's closed down the whorehouses and they're costing him his miners."

Clint remembered the old geezer outside the saloon earlier that morning.

"His miners are deserting him and new ones won't come here. Not with the prospect of no women and with the even worse prospect of no liquor."

"No liquor?"

The sheriff nodded.

"That's what the Citizen's Committee is threatening to do next—to make the whole town dry, with very stiff penalties for anyone who so much as even talks about having a drink—and I'd have to carry it out."

The sheriff's disgust was clearly evident.

"Sounds like the Committee is getting out of hand."

"Just the way any group does when its basic elements are fear and misunderstanding."

"But if the murders were stopped, the Committee would lose its power?"

"Hopefully."

"What are the chances of finding the killer?"

Before the lawman could answer there was a sudden burst of shouting outside in the corridor. Clint turned and looked up just as a man with a flowing white mane of hair, burning blue eyes and a parson's black suit and white collar pushed his way into the office.

"This," the Sheriff said to Clint, "is Parson Robeson."

SIX

"I've just been informed that another dead prostitute has been brought to Riley's Mortuary, Sheriff."

Sheriff Halsey looked miserable.

"I'm afraid that's the case, Parson."

"Do you realize what this means?"

"It means we've got another murder on our hands."

"Oh ho, it means more than that, my good man. Far more!"

Clint guessed that the parson was in his early forties. He had the look of a man who kept himself in good shape. He also had the look of a man who was skilled in getting his way. His voice was deep and polished, like that of an orator seeking office.

Another man had come into the office with him, dressed in a dark suit, but he looked like no clergyman Clint had ever seen. Clint thought this man would be more at home with a gun on his hip. He stood to one side and remained silent throughout Robeson's diatribe.

"I mean," the parson said, "that we will most definitely seek your removal from office immediately—well before the election. We can't have our town at the mercy of an insane killer whom our elected sheriff is incapable of catching!" As he finished speaking, he glanced down at Clint. "A murderer is walking about loose while you sit passing the time—with this man, whoever he is."

"This," Sheriff Halsey said, obviously knowing the impact of his words, "is Clint Adams, Parson—better known as the Gunsmith."

Recognition dawned on the parson's face immediately.

"You mean to say that this is the Gunsmith—the infamous gunfighter?"

"I wouldn't call him a gunfighter, exactly, or infamous," Halsey said, knowing Clint's background as a lawman, but the parson was off on another diatribe without listening.

"Is it not enough that alcohol flows like water in our streets—not enough that girls scarcely old enough to enter grammar school sell themselves to the highest bidder—now we have a notorious gunfighter in our midst! What next, Sheriff? What next?"

Sheriff Halsey stood up. His face was red, his eyes angry.

"I think I've had enough of this, Parson. I've conducted myself like a gentleman up until now, tolerating your outbursts, but I don't know how much longer I can guarantee such behavior. Now, I'd like you to leave my office."

The parson surprised Clint by standing up to Halsey.

"Oh, I'll leave, Sheriff—for now. But I can assure you that I'll be back, armed with the full power of the Committee, and asking—demanding—your resignation!"

With that he glared down at Clint and then stormed out of the room.

"Who was the man with him?"

"That's his assistant, Jordan. I don't think I've ever heard the man speak. He just stands off to one side and watches the Parson."

"His companion looked more like a bodyguard than an assistant, to me," Clint observed.

Clint leaned forward, taking from his pocket the note that Sally Raines had told him about during her dying moments.

"I didn't want to discuss this until we were alone, Sheriff."

Clint stood up and walked over to close the door. He then handed the sheriff the note.

The sheriff read it and then looked up at Clint.

"You have any idea what this means?"

"Nothing more than that it led Sally Raines straight here—possibly into a trap!"

"You don't think this note is legitimate, that someone really does know who the killer is?"

Clint shook his head.

"I think that whoever killed her friend Helen also sent the note to Sally."

"Why would the killer do that?"

"Sally Raines was also a prostitute."

"You may be right, Clint," Halsey said, rubbing his jaw. "You may be right." He handed the note back and asked, "What are your plans?"

"Well, if you don't mind I think I'd like to stick around and help you find your murderer."

The sheriff grinned like a small boy.

"Mind? I'm flattered—and grateful. I'm going to need all the help I can get to withstand the Committee."

When Clint left the sheriff's office he took his rig and Duke to the livery stable where a teenager with strawberry freckles walked around and around Duke in awe and agreed to take care of both the rig and the horse until further notice.

Next Clint went in search of a hotel, finding one, the Amboy, where for two dollars a night he found pleasant room and board. In the lobby he looked at the playbills advertising roving minstrels and entertainers, among whom he was surprised to find one of his favorites, a comedian named Rubber Face, who he had once seen in Chicago.

After a shave, bath and a big breakfast of bacon, eggs and big slabs of toasted rye bread, Clint went looking for the reporter named Graves.

He found the little man in the checkered suit in an obviously embarrassing situation. Carrying a carpetbag in one hand and several writing tablets in another, Graves stood out in front of a boarding house, arguing with a heavy woman who had a rolling pin in one fat fist.

"You just try and get back in here without paying your rent, Mr. Graves, and see what happens!"

"I told you, dear lady, that I would pay you as soon as my check arrives from London."

"Check! Ha!" the woman scoffed. "I took it upon myself to look through your mail, Mr. Graves, and I just happened to come across a letter from your publisher saying that he was sick and tired of your wild goose chases and that you should consider yourself off his payroll—permanently! You won't be getting any more paychecks, Mr. Graves, so don't be giving me any of your stuff."

"I've money coming, I tell you."

"Ha!"

Clint noted that, ironically, although the woman clearly disliked Graves, she continued to address him as "mister," probably because he wore a tie. People from the working classes sometimes seemed cowed by the most superficial of symbols.

Clint assessed the crumbling house and decided that rent here couldn't be that much. He reached into his pocket and stepped forward.

"How much is his rent?"

Both Graves and the woman had been so intent on their argument that they hadn't noticed Clint.

"What?" the woman asked.

"I want to know how much he owes you."

"And why would you want to know that?"

"I'd say that was my business."

"Are you a friend of his?" she said incredulously, as if the little man could not possibly have any friends.

"How much?" Clint asked again.

She told him. Clint handed her the money.

Both Graves and the woman looked astonished— and a little suspicious.

"Now," Clint said to Graves, "you can go and put your things back in your room."

Hesitantly, as if he didn't know if he was awake or dreaming, Graves said, "Yes, all right."

"Just who are you?" the woman demanded as Graves disappeared into the house.

"It doesn't matter."

"It matters to me."

"Why?" Clint asked. "Money's money, isn't it? That's all you need worry about."

"He's a bad investment, that one, I'm warning you," she said, with a knowing look. "He's got only one thing on his mind. It's always the Ripper this and

the Ripper that. The other boarders avoid him like
the plague. He's . . . odd!"

When Graves reappeared Clint thanked her very
much for the information and then said to Graves,
"Come on, I'll buy you some breakfast."

Graves turned to the woman. "I'll be back later,"
he said, as if with great satisfaction. Then he turned
to Clint.

"What's this all about?" Graves asked. "Do I
know you from somewhere?"

"I need some information."

"About what."

"About your Ripper, Mr. Graves."

SEVEN

The killer cleaned the surgical knife in lye and water and wiped it carefully on a clean towel, looking at the blade with respect.

With this knife justice was being done.

With this knife people, sinful people, people who deserved to die horribly, would soon learn the error of the lives they led.

The killer lay the knife back in the satin-lined box where it would rest until next time.

Until tonight.

EIGHT

From the quick, noisy way he ate it was obvious that it had been some time since Graves' last decent meal. Along with three eggs and two slices of ham thick enough to sole shoes with, the little man also had three well-buttered pieces of toast.

When he finished he ordered another pot of coffee and then sat back and took the stub of a cigar from his pocket. In his filthy checkered suit and faded derby he looked like a caricature of a hobo.

"I'd like you to tell me what you've found out about the killings, so far," Clint said.

Graves blew smoke into the air and said, "I'll tell you one thing for sure. I think the Ripper's operating right here in Dante."

"You're sure of that?"

Graves seemed offended.

"I walked the foggy streets of Whitechapel on nights when even Scotland Yard was afraid to go out. I stalked my man and if it hadn't been for an obtuse

35

police captain, I would have had him, too."

"What obtuse police captain?"

"The one who said that the types of papers I wrote for did not qualify me as a journalist. I therefore had to drop my investigation or be threatened with a charge of what is called an obstruction of justice."

Until now Clint had been somewhat amused by the small man. Now he grew serious.

"You don't really think that the Ripper is here, do you, Graves?"

Graves inhaled more smoke.

"Does that idea scare you?"

"No, it makes me think that maybe I've wasted the price of a breakfast."

Graves eyed his small stack of empty plates.

"I certainly appreciate it, Cap'n, and I also appreciate your putting up my rent money. You can be sure that you'll get it back. As soon as I prove that the Ripper's out here, I'll have to beat the newspapers away with a stick."

Clint said, "You didn't answer my question."

"What's that?"

"I asked if you really believed that the Ripper was in Dante, or are you just trying to get yourself some publicity."

"No, sir. I really believe it. He's here, all right. I can feel him. I can *smell* him."

"Why would he choose to come here?"

"A mining town's a great place for a man like the Ripper. Plenty of prostitution and a big enough population to hide in."

"So you think that the Ripper is actually living in Dante?"

"Yes, and I think I even know where."

Graves had spoken his last words with a flourish. Obviously, he expected a shocked response from Clint but the tall man only smiled.

"You're worse than Ned Buntline."

"Buntline! Bah! A dreary hack!"

"And what are you?"

Graves patted himself on the chest.

"An artist, a seeker of truth."

"I see."

"Your skepticism is starting to aggravate me, sir."

"I feel much the same way about all of your crazy talk. You mentioned knowing where the 'Ripper' lives. Why haven't you told the sheriff?"

This time Graves offered no flourish.

"I consider the sheriff a prime suspect," he said, speaking very seriously.

"Of being the Ripper?" Clint asked in surprise.

"No, but maybe of committing one or two of the murders and making them look like the Ripper's work."

"Why would you suspect the sheriff?"

"He beats female prisoners—and he beats them pretty badly."

"You know this for a fact?"

"I know one of the women he's beaten. A prostitute named Darla. We could go and visit her and she could tell you herself."

Clint finished his coffee.

"Not until you tell me who you suspect of being the real Ripper."

Graves leaned forward, as if he were divulging a dangerous secret. His eyes darted furtively about the restaurant.

"His name is Fredric K. Carver. 'Carver.' Get it?"

"As in carved up?"

"Exactly!"

"Why do you suspect him? Surely you have a better reason than just his name."

Now Graves sat back in his chair.

"Because despite the best efforts of the esteemed

sheriff, I roam the streets at night. The night of the second murder, I was no more than a block away from where the killing took place. I chased the killer several blocks before he eluded me in the fog. But he left something behind that he will come to regret."

"What's that?"

"His footprint. I went back in the daylight to retrace my steps just in case I might find something like that."

"And how does that lead to Mr. Carver?"

"We can check Carver's foot with it and see."

"I still don't understand why you suspect him."

"Because he's a man of mystery. I met someone who shares the same boarding house with Carver in a bar a few weeks ago. He told me about him. Nobody ever sees him come in or go out. I think he only goes out at night—to kill. Look, why don't you come along with me?"

"Where?"

"To the boarding house where Fredric Carver lives."

Clint stared at the little man and then said, "You're really serious, aren't you?"

"So serious I could well be putting both our lives in jeopardy."

"You know how I like it," the miner said.

He was drunk enough already this morning to risk arrest for coming over to Selena's famous house of ill repute. Downstairs he'd argued loudly with Selena. He wanted Jessica. All the men wanted Jessica. Finally, Selena relented.

Now twenty-five year old Jessica Ames stood next to the bed in her second floor room and let her silk nightgown fall to the floor, revealing sumptuous firm young breasts.

The miner groaned at the sight of her.

Now she walked closer, to show the brilliant black of her bush.

"You know you're not supposed to be here, don't you?" she asked. "All the little houses of fun are officially closed down."

But the miner only groaned some more, roughly removed his own clothes, and then walked over to her, led by a big, almost comic erection.

He pushed her back on the bed. She knew exactly what to do. First she kissed his chest, edging down on her until she took him in her hands and then put him in her mouth. As she worked on him he thrashed around on the bed like he was losing his mind.

Finally, she climbed on top of him, sliding down his rigid cock. He filled his hands with her breasts as she started to ride him until he exploded inside of her.

"There," she said, immediately after he'd had his orgasm, easing herself off of him and the bed. He tried to grab her to hug her, but she eluded him. They paid for an orgasm, and with beautiful Jessica that's just what they got—and that's all.

He seemed dazed now as well as drunk and she helped him on with his clothes and led him out the door.

When she was alone again she went over to the washbasin and cleaned herself up. She used the soap gratefully, as if it were a life-saving medicine. Finally she perfumed herself, lifted the lid off her music box so that it played the pretty Stephen Foster tune that she liked so much, and then she sat in a rocker in front of the window and stared at the sky. A few minutes later there was a knock at her door.

Selena entered when Jessica called out permission.

"I'm sorry, but he insisted that it be you and no one else," Selena said.

Jessica smiled.

"It's all right. I haven't been making much money lately anyhow. At least he was quick about it."

Selena, who was in her mid-fifties, fleshy and given to smoking cigars, said, "It's almost a curse, isn't it, Jessica?"

"What?" the younger woman asked.

"Being as lovely as you are."

"I suppose it is, sometimes."

Selena came over and stood by Jessica's rocker.

"What are you looking at?"

"Just the blue sky."

Selena shook her head sadly and said, "You're still thinking of Arlette, aren't you?"

"Yes, I suppose I am."

"That bastard."

"Maybe we should talk about something else."

"They'll catch him, Jessica. Wait and see. They'll catch him and he'll hang for what he did to Arlette and the others, and we'll all be there to see it."

Jessica continued to stare at the sky. Arlette had been her best friend, and now Arlette was dead, ripped savagely apart by a mindless killer.

"I'd like to be alone for awhile, Selena, if that's all right."

"Sure, Jessie honey, sure, but if you want to talk, you just call old Selena, all right?"

"Yes, thank you."

As Selena left she looked back at Jessica, who was rocking very slowly, her eyes still fixed on the sky.

NINE

Twenty minutes later Clint and Graves stood in front of a three-story rooming house. On the porch sat a few older men in remnants of Union uniforms. They smoked corncob pipes and bit off chaws of tobacco and stared curiously at Clint and Rupert Graves. They seemed to have a lot to say to each other about Graves' checkered suit.

"This where Carver lives?" Clint asked.

Graves nodded.

"Come on. We'll go and talk to the landlady."

Clint smiled.

"You don't seem to have much luck with landladies."

They went up the steps, past the old timers, and knocked on the door.

"Out back, if you're looking for Mrs. Haynes," a toothless old man said.

They went around to the back. Sheets fluttered in the wind like the sails of schooner ships. The air seemed bleached clean. Amidst the sheets they found a squat, stolid woman.

"Mrs. Haynes?"

"Yes."

"We'd like to ask you a few questions about one of your boarders."

She looked at them skeptically.

"You with the law?"

"A friend of mine was stabbed to death last night," Clint said evenly. "I'm led to believe that one of your boarders might know something about it."

Compassion shone in the woman's eyes.

"Your friend is dead?"

"Yes, she is."

"Which boarder do you want to know about?"

"A Mr. Carver."

Now something new played in her eyes.

"Oh, yes, Mr. Carver."

"What's wrong, Mrs. Haynes?"

"Oh, nothing."

Clint advanced a step.

"If there's something you'd like to say, Mrs. Haynes, please do. It could be important."

"It's just about Mr. Carver . . ."

"Yes?"

"You know, I've never actually seen the man. He rented the room by sending a bank draft in an envelope from Denver. He came in in the middle of the night. Since then he only comes and goes late at night when I'm sleeping, or at dawn. He also made it clear that he doesn't want anyone to go into his room to tidy. So we never go in—just leave clean sheets and towels outside the door."

"That's strange," Clint said.

"Very strange. But he pays his rent."

"Have any of the other boarders seen him?"

"No, but they sure talk about him plenty. They're

as curious about him as I am."

Clint said, "I'd really like to see his room."

"I'm not sure that would be right."

"Is he in?"

"Not right now."

"Would you let me see the room?"

"I don't know—"

"Sheriff Halsey will vouch for me."

"You a friend of Burt's?"

"In a way we're working together."

She looked at Clint closely.

"For some reason, young man, I trust you."

"Thank you, Ma'am," Clint said, although it had been a long time since he'd been called "young man."

The room was on the third floor, at the top of a pair of winding stairways and at the end of a narrow hallway. One thing he had to say for Mrs. Haynes, every inch of her house was spotless and smelled clean.

After knocking just to be on the safe side she took a cluster of keys from her house dress, chose the right one and opened the door.

Behind Clint, Graves gasped at what he saw. For his part, Clint could only stand and stare. Covering the walls were clippings from London newspapers with headlines proclaiming RIPPER STRIKES AGAIN! and RIPPER KILLS MORE!

Mrs. Haynes brought a hand to her bosom. Her eyes were wide with fear.

"My Lord!" she gasped.

"Mrs. Haynes," Clint said gently, "could you have someone go and get the sheriff?"

"Yes, of course . . ." she said, and backed out of the room.

While they waited for the sheriff, Clint and

Graves went through the room.

The place seemed to be a shrine to the Ripper. Magazines, books, and stacks of newspapers were jammed into virtually every available space. What ordinary items there were—clothing and a few valises—lay sprawled on the bed, untouched.

"I'd say we found his lair," Graves said. "Yes, sir, the lair of the Ripper himself!"

Graves was rubbing his hands together gleefully, but Clint was not prepared to accept the situation at face value so easily.

"Let's wait and see," he said.

TEN

Colonel Thomas Porter looked out the window of his mansion on the edge of Dante and said, "They're out there again, Ling Chi."

Ling Chi, a handsome Chinese man of about sixty, stepped up next to his employer and looked out.

"Parson Robeson is at work again," he said in barely accented English.

Colonel Porter, a huge man who managed to make all attire look military, took a stogie from his mouth and said, "You know what he's doing, don't you?"

"Robeson?"

"Yes."

"Trying to secure himself the mayorship, I would imagine."

"Exactly. That's what whipping up the mob is all about. So they'll vote for him a few years from now when he 'suddenly' decides to run."

Porter jabbed his cigar at the demonstrators who

walked up and down in front of his house.

DOWN WITH SIN! one sign read.

DOWN WITH THE COLONEL! reads another.

A third said, FREE DANTE OF SINFUL WOMEN!

"I've closed down the pleasure houses," Porter said, "what more do they want?"

"I think they want you to *really* put them out of business," Ling Chi said, referring to the fact that the house still did some business, "unofficially." "Also, they might want you to close down the saloons."

"Then I might as well close down the mines, too. Without women *or* whiskey we'd never get anyone to work here. How about this, Ling? I'll close the mines and in a few years Robeson can run for mayor —of a ghost town!"

Ling Chi moved to stare out the window again, but jerked back quickly as a rock smashed against the window pane. The glass did not break, but the intent was obvious.

"The parson really wants a war," Porter said.

"It is because of the killings," Ling said. "He paints them as being a logical consequence to sin."

"Then dammit, I want this killer caught!"

"The sheriff does not seem to have many leads." Ling Chi's eyes brightened. "I did receive an interesting piece of news this morning."

"What's that?"

"A man named Clint Adams has come to town."

"The Gunsmith? In Dante?"

"Yes. He was with the woman who was killed last night. Now he too stalks the killer."

The colonel jabbed at the air with his cigar.

"Get him here, Ling. Get him here as soon as you can."

• • •

"Blood," Clint said, as he felt along the side of the closet.

"Here," Sheriff Halsey said. He handed Clint a kerosene lamp.

Clint closely examined the closet floor and found two drops of a red, sticky substance.

He stood up, handing the lamp back and rolling the stuff between two fingers of his other hand.

"I'd say this blood isn't more than twelve hours old."

"Then it probably came from the knife that killed your friend, Sally Raines," Halsey said.

"Probably."

Sheriff Halsey turned back to the walls decorated with Ripper mementos.

"This is worse than I thought."

"How's that?" Clint asked.

Halsey glared at Graves. It was obvious that the two men were in no danger of becoming friends.

"Maybe Graves here is right. Maybe the Ripper did come over here from London."

"I'd like to know where he is," Graves said. "Nobody sees him. The boarders only *hear* him occasionally, going out and coming in. Where does he go and what does he do when he's not killing?"

Clint smiled bitterly.

"If we knew that, we'd know where to go and get him."

ELEVEN

The killer stood on the corner watching as women scurried from the general store to other available shops. Late at night prostitutes liked to stroll this area of town near the saloons.

It was ideal for what the killer had in mind for tonight.

Ideal.

TWELVE

As Clint was leaving the boarding house with Graves and the sheriff, a sleek black wagon pulled up to the boardwalk and stopped. A Chinese man of great dignity turned to Clint from the driver's seat and asked, "Are you the man known as the Gunsmith, sir?"

"Yes."

"Then would you be so kind as to join me?"

"You're being summoned into the presence," the sheriff noted.

"Parson Robeson?" Clint asked.

Halsey shook his head.

"Colonel Porter."

"I wonder why."

"The colonel isn't the type to mince words. You'll find out soon enough."

Clint said to the Chinese man, "I'll come with you. Just give me a moment."

"As you wish, sir."

He turned to face both Graves and the sheriff.

"I hope the three of us can work together from now on." He spoke for the benefit of both the sheriff and Graves. "We'll be able to accomplish a hell of a lot more that way."

The sheriff smiled.

"I guess I don't see why not."

Graves—being Graves—spoiled the moment by saying, "Then would you mind buying me a cup of coffee?"

The sheriff stared at him for a moment and then, to Clint's relief, laughed and looked at Clint.

"He isn't an easy man to like."

"I didn't say we had to like each other," Clint said, "just work together."

With that he boarded the wagon and waved to both of them. As the wagon pulled away they fell into a heated discussion. Clint hoped they wouldn't come to blows while he was gone.

Sheriff Halsey hadn't been exaggerating. After offering brandy, which Clint refused in favor of coffee, Colonel Porter turned away from the window of his study and got right down to business.

"Personally, I think the parson is behind these killings."

"That's quite an accusation."

"The man has ambitions. I think he's trying to create a mood of desperation, of despair, and then show the people that he is their only way out. He and his people are obsessed with 'morality,'" he continued. "They'd be glad to be rid of me and my miners."

"That wouldn't leave much of a town for them to live in."

"That's exactly what I said."

"You think the parson would go so far as to kill

five women to get what he wants?"

"The man's a madman," the colonel said with feeling. "He doesn't see prostitutes as women, he sees them as 'vessels of the devil.'"

Clint sipped his coffee and listened to the man intently. He felt comfortable with the colonel.

"When I heard you were in Dante I couldn't believe my luck. You're exactly the man we need to catch this maniac." He lit a huge cigar after Clint declined one. "You can catch the Ripper. You'll want to when you hear my offer."

"I already want to, Colonel."

"Hear me out. I'll give you five thousand dollars to find this madman and bring him to justice."

Clint held up his hand.

"First of all, Colonel, I don't want your money. I came to Dante because a woman I knew briefly was murdered almost in my presence and I feel I owe it to her to find her killer. Secondly, I don't want in any way to undermine your sheriff."

"Don't misunderstand me," the colonel said. "Halsey is a good enough man for the normal problems in a town like this. But these murders seem to have him stumped. I'm worried that by the time the killer is apprehended the parson's group will have voted the town dry and driven off what's left of my miners."

Clint helped himself to more coffee. The colonel had said it was Colombian, but Clint only knew that it was the most delicious coffee he'd ever had. He liked coffee with a strong, hard bite, and this filled the order.

"I'm working on a few ideas, Colonel. Hopefully they'll pan out before the Ripper strikes again."

"Even you're calling him the 'Ripper,'" the colonel said in exasperation. "I'll tell you what. Let me at least cover your expenses: your hotel, your meals, and any other money that you might have to spend while looking for this killer. I can at least do that."

Clint thought a moment and then said, "All right. That sounds fair."

He stood up and put out his hand and the colonel stepped forward and took it.

"Don't forget what I said about the parson. There's more to that man than meets the eye."

"I'll keep that in mind. It was good meeting you, Colonel."

"And you, sir. I feel much better just knowing you're here."

Clint left hoping he'd be able to justify the colonel's confidence.

THIRTEEN

Clint stood in front of the sedate brick three-story house which even had a captain's walk. He had to hand it to the colonel. Most men would not think to make a cat house look so respectable.

The note inviting Sally Raines to Dante burned in Clint's pocket. It only made sense to ask other ladies of the same profession if they'd known Sally. Maybe one of them had. Maybe one of them knew who had written her the note—or had written it themselves.

Clint knocked at the door. In moments a tired-looking woman in her fifties answered. He was surprised to see that she was chewing tobacco.

"Yes?"

"Good afternoon, Ma'am," he said, politely. "My name is Clint Adams—"

"And mine's Selena," the woman said. "What does that get us?"

"I'd like to talk to you for a moment, if I can."

"Honey, maybe you don't read the local newspapers or hear too good. The parson has seen to it that we are closed down." She punctuated her remark by letting go with a stream of brown tobacco juice past Clint into the street.

"That's never stopped a good house from operating before."

"Oh, once in a while one of our regulars manages to sneak in and I've got to let him go upstairs before he raises too much of a ruckus, but for the most part we don't dare go against the parson." She nodded across the street. "One of his people could be watching us right now."

Clint looked across the street. Behind a lace curtain he could see a forehead and a pair of eyes.

"Last night a woman named Sally Raines was stabbed to death near my wagon."

"Yeah, I heard about it."

"Somebody wrote her a note telling her to come to Dante if she wanted to find out who killed her friend. I would like to try and find out if any of your girls knew Sally."

"Not that anybody's mentioned."

"I'm wondering if I could talk with the girls."

"You could try, honey, but it wouldn't do you a lot of good."

"Why is that?"

"Because my girls figure that the further away from the killings they stay, the better off they'll be. I kind of support their thinking."

Clint's jaw muscles clenched. He couldn't stomach such apathy in the face of what was going on.

"I'm hoping to find the killer, Ma'am. In order to do that I'll need your cooperation and the cooperation of your girls."

Selena cocked her head to one side and asked, "Are you the law?"

Clint shook his head.

"Just a citizen who doesn't like to see young women get cut up."

"Most people don't give a damn one way or another about what happens to whores."

Just behind the woman, in the vestibule, Clint thought he caught sight of a lovely woman's face, but it was gone before he could be sure.

"So you won't help?"

"Afraid not."

"I would think that you especially would want this killer caught."

She spat a stream of tobacco juice again, as ably as any man.

"Maybe it's time for old Selena to move on. Maybe this is fate calling me. Maybe I'll just head out for California, or someplace."

"There's some hard times out there, too."

"California?"

"Everywhere."

"That's what I hear." She smiled at him with tobacco-stained teeth. "Somehow men find money for whores, even if their families have to go hungry."

With an outlook like that "old" Selena was certainly not in danger of becoming one of Clint Adams' all time favorite people.

He nodded coldly to the madam and walked away.

Graves sat in Sheriff Halsey's office with his feet up on the desk and a cup of coffee in his hands.

Ever since Graves had met Clint Adams a few hours ago his fortunes had taken a turn for the better. His rent had been paid, he'd had his first good meal in weeks, and now the sheriff was letting him hang around in the office and assist with the investigation.

What a strange thing destiny was. Less than four hours ago Graves had been nothing more than the flotsam he'd been all of his life.

Now he was somebody.

He put down his coffee and decided to take a stroll back among the cells, where the prisoners were kept. If there was a prisoner there, maybe he'd tell him how he was somebody, now.

FOURTEEN

"Mister! Mister! Wait!"

Clint had just turned the corner down from Selena's cathouse when as fetching a sight as he had ever seen came running down the alley towards him.

He recognized her face instantly. It was the one he thought he had seen fleetingly in the vestibule behind Selena. He was willing to bet she was also the one he had seen at the window.

"What can I do for you?"

"I think I can help you, about Sally Raines, I mean."

"Come on, then. We'll have some coffee and talk about it."

"We can't, Mister."

"Why not?"

"Because the parson has decreed that none of us girls can ever go into respectable establishments even to shop, let alone to eat or have coffee."

Clint smiled.

"Let's just say that I don't count myself as being among the parson's flock."

She grinned. She was a raven-haired beauty with delicate and melancholy features.

"Come on," he said, taking her by the arm. "I'll buy you a whole lunch."

Why not, he thought. Colonel Porter would be paying the check.

"No, really, Mister. I wouldn't want to be the cause of a scene. I couldn't take being called names, and that's what the parson's people do to you around here."

"My name's Clint. What's yours?"

"Jessica, Jessica Ames."

"Well, Jessica Ames, I'm going to make it my number one priority of the day to make sure that nobody calls you any names. Okay?"

"I'd really rather talk . . . somewhere private."

"Well," he said, hesitantly, "we could go to my room—if you don't mind that."

She actually seemed relieved.

"I don't mind."

"They say I was drunk but that's just bullshit. Bullshit!"

The rotund man speaking was long innocent of razor or soap. Even now, a full day after his arrest for being drunk and disorderly, he reeked of alcohol.

He stood on the other side of the bars. Graves had to keep his distance, the man's odor was so bad.

"You a lawyer?" the man demanded of Graves.

"No, I am not a lawyer."

"Then how come you're back here strollin' down the cellblock?"

Graves was only more than happy to tell him—to tell someone!

"I happen to be a good friend of the sheriff's."

"Then you're no durned friend of mine!" the drunk yelled. "And I'll thank you kindly to remove yourself from my sight!"

Which, given the man's odor, Graves was only too happy to do.

Graves had once spent a night in a London jail. He'd never forgotten the experience. He'd felt torn between fear and pity—fear of some of the truly frightening creatures he encountered there, and pity for the pathetic ones. Not even the hospitals brimmed over with human misery as much as jails did.

Graves thought of all this as he passed down the cell block, half a dozen faces looking out at him as he passed. Some scowled at him, some smirked, some just stared blankly—too lost in their own grief to pay any attention to him.

At the end of the cellblock he saw a pug-nosed young man curled up in the corner of his bunk, something unlikely in his hands.

A rosary.

Graves went over and took a closer look. Where the other prisoners tended to group together, to call insults and trade information, this man was totally withdrawn. In his torn white shirt and dark trousers, his auburn hair mussed, he was not handsome, but he did look to be of a superior intelligence to the others in this place.

Graves, with a reporter's hunch, decided to ask the man about the rosary.

"Are you praying for all the other lost souls in this place, or are you praying for yourself?"

When the young man looked up at him, Graves saw in the gaze something he'd not seen since an experience he'd had in London.

The man said nothing.

"Don't be frightened," Graves said.

"Who are you?" the boy asked. "Are you a priest?"

Graves laughed.

"Oh no, son, I'm no priest, believe me."

"Then who are you?"

Graves started to say that he was a friend of the sheriff's again but for some reason he stopped.

Instead he said, "Let's just say that I know you didn't do what they say you did—and I want to help you."

"You're a lawyer, then?"

Graves shrugged.

"Something like that, yes."

"Then you're familiar with my case?"

"Yes," Graves lied, "but I wish you'd go over the particulars, just so I'm sure I have all of the details straight."

The details were simple enough: The young man had suffered from headaches most of his life. Lately, as he neared age twenty, he started having spells. There were some—especially the parson's people— who said that he was possessed by demons. Last night some of the men he worked with on the railroad, it being payday and all, had given him some corn liquor. The young man, Gil Evars, had gone berserk and smashed up a bar. He awoke this morning to find himself in jail, accused of having stolen another worker's pay check.

"I do remember smashing the place up, that's how I get with these headaches. But I know I never stole no money. That ain't like me. I was raised on the Bible and that just ain't like me."

At this point, however, Graves was hardly listening. He let him babble on.

Graves had conceived grand plans for the both of them—starting very soon.

When Evars finally stopped talking Graves said, "You've got my sympathy, son. You surely do."

"How long do you think they'll keep me in here? I've never been in jail before."

"Not long, son. I'll see to that."

"You will?" Evars said, jumping to his feet and grabbing the bars. Tears of gratitude shone in his eyes. "You're going to help me?"

"Yes, son," Graves said. "I'm going to help you."

Then he smiled, thinking to himself: But I'm going to help myself even more. For now, he was in a hurry to leave the cell block.

He needed to see Colonel Porter.

Soon.

FIFTEEN

Of course, when he suggested that they go to his room he really had no intentions of taking Jessica to bed. She *was* incredibly beautiful, but his intention had been to get her to relax so that they could talk comfortably.

As they entered the room she began to prowl restlessly.

"Jessica—"

"You don't know what it's like having sex with strange men, doing what they want me to do, for money."

He decided to remain silent and let her talk, as it might help her relax.

"I can't remember the last time I had sex just for the pure pleasure of it, with a sweet, tender man."

She turned and looked at him then, and her gaze was speculative.

"My God," she said, covering her face, "there's a

maniac out there killing girls and I'm thinking about going to bed with you."

"It's all right," he said, moving towards her and taking hold of her shoulders. "I'm thinking about going to bed with you, too."

"Really? It's funny, isn't it? I . . . sense that you would be gentle. You're not like the men who come to Selena's. You don't go to whorehouses, do you?"

"No."

"I didn't think so," she said, backing away from him. "You probably wouldn't want to touch me."

"Jessica, I think you're one of the most beautiful, desirable women I've ever met, and I'd like very much to go to bed with you . . . but I wouldn't want to take advantage of you in a vulnerable state."

"I'm not vulnerable, Clint," she said, moving closer to him again and taking his hand. She brought his hand to her cheek and said, "I'm just afraid I've forgotten how to . . . make love."

She stared at him, her cheek against his hand, and he felt himself responding. She turned her face so that her mouth came into contact with his palm and he felt her tongue flick out.

"Jessica—"

"I'm sorry," she said, sliding her arms around his neck, "I'm sorry . . ."

She got up on her toes and pushed her mouth against his. As he closed his arms around her he could feel her urgency causing her body to tremble. Her lips were sweet, her tongue eager.

He unbuttoned her shirt so he could slide his hands over her marvelous breasts. They were large and well-rounded, heavy in his hand, just the way he liked them. Abruptly, he slid the shirt down around her waist and leaned forward to kiss her breasts, suckle her nipples.

"Ooh, yes . . ." she said, cupping his head and

pulling his face against her.

Her skin was so smooth and fragrant that he lost himself in its scent and feel.

"The bed, Clint, please, let's go to bed."

They walked to the bed and fell on it together. They discarded their clothing quickly and came together urgently.

Her hands surrounded his cock and she stroked it lovingly.

"No whore tricks," she whispered to him, "I just want to make love . . ."

And so did he. Everything else was forgotten now that he was in bed with this incredibly lovely, sweet-smelling beauty.

He attacked her breasts with his mouth while she continued to hold his penis, stroking it gently. She made him shiver when she ran her nails along the underside.

He began to explore her body with his mouth now, reluctantly abandoning her breasts, moving down over the slight hill of her belly until his face was nestled in her fragrant bush. His tongue flicked out, tasting her salty nectar and then plunging into her. She brought her hips up to meet the pressure of his tongue and held the back of his head with her hands while he sucked and lapped her into a frenzy, until finally she came with a loud cry. . .

He climbed atop her then and slid his rigid cock into her slowly, until he was buried to the hilt. They began moving together then, seeking a tempo that would satisfy both of them, and when they did they went on like that for a long time, enjoying each other until finally neither one of them could hold back.

After they made love Clint finally convinced Jessica to go out with him for lunch.

"After all," he said, "I think we've both worked up an appetite."

She couldn't argue with that.

Clint had decided on the Eldorado House because Jessica told him they served the best food in town. She also told him nervously that it was where they would most likely encounter Parson Robeson.

Clint's mouth began to water as he contemplated the menu at the Eldorado. He finally ordered ham, mashed potatoes and corn. Jessica chose fried chicken.

"I know that Marcie knew this Sally Raines," Jessica confided to Clint.

"Marcie is one of the girls back at Selena's?"

Jessica nodded.

"That's why I wanted to talk to you. So I could tell you about Marcie."

"I appreciate it."

Jessica's lovely eyes were heavy with sadness. The waitress arrived, laden down with their dinner plates, biscuits and coffee.

"I've known them all," Jessica continued after they'd eaten in silence for a while.

"All the women who were killed?"

"Yes."

"I'm sorry."

She looked down at her coffee.

"When I heard about Sally Raines I just started to tremble."

"We'll catch him."

"I hope so."

"You don't sound very confident."

"The sheriff's been saying he was going to catch this killer for three months, now."

"I have a feeling we're closer to the killer then ever before, though."

Clint was about to go on when he sensed a presence behind him. When he turned to look up he saw a burning blue gaze and a mane of white hair.

Parson Robeson.

"May I ask you, sir," Robeson said in a calm but theatrical voice, "to cast an eye around this eating establishment."

Clint obliged him by looking around. The place was filled with people having lunch.

"Nice place," Clint said, and turned his back on the Parson.

"That is not my point," Robeson said.

Clint turned again and stared at him.

"Then maybe you'd be so kind as to tell me what your point is?"

"As you look around this place, what you see are many of this town's most respectable citizens having lunch."

"And a very good lunch it is, too. I recommend the ham, Parson."

"I would like to emphasize the word 'respectable.'"

"Go ahead, emphasize it."

The parson appeared speechless for a moment. This confrontation was not going the way he had planned.

Clint could see that Jessica had tensed up, shoulders hunched and her eyes tearful.

"All right, Parson, I believe I know the point you're trying to make. If it's all the same to you, though, I'd prefer that you try to make it somewhere else, to someone else. We haven't finished our lunch yet and we don't want it to get cold. I don't have time for your pompous foolishness."

Robeson tensed up, his face growing red, and he pointed an accusatory finger at Jessica.

"She is a whore!"

"And you're an annoying sonofabitch, Parson," Clint said, pleasantly. "Now that we got that settled why don't you take a walk?"

Before the parson could reply a chunky young man in a three piece suit appeared behind him. He smelled of sweet cologne, had a nose that had been hammered more than once and the sour expression of a bully. Clint wondered where the Parson's "assistant" with the gunman's eyes was.

"What the Parson means to say is that we don't want women who stink of the whorehouse sitting with our wives and daughters."

Clint's fist crashed into the man's face before he could utter another word. Then Clint caught him with an uppercut that sent the man sprawling over the table where he had been sitting with two other men overturning dishes and glasses. The man lay there, eyes dazed and mouth cut and bleeding.

His companions, who tempered their anger with fear, grabbed the man and kept him from standing up.

Clint addressed the restaurant at large.

"Now, before I sit down and finish my meal I want to know if there's anyone else who objects to this lady and I being here?"

There was a lot of general muttering, but nobody said anything.

Clint then glared at Parson Robeson and said, "You better take that walk."

"You have not heard the last of this, Mr. Adams. Not by a long sight."

"I have this afternoon, Parson. Goodbye."

Clint turned his back on the Parson and sat back down at his table. The man he knocked down was helped outside by his friends, and the parson soon followed.

"It sounds like blackmail to me!" Colonel Thomas Porter said.

Rupert Graves sat on the other side of Porter's vast desk, patiently waiting for the man to regain control of his temper.

"Your mining operations are virtually a shambles," Graves said carefully when Porter fell silent. "If I can find the Ripper, then everything will go back to normal and everyone will benefit."

"But if you know the identity of the man already why not tell me—or the Sheriff—now?"

Graves shook his head.

"I didn't say that I knew the man's identity, Colonel. I said I was working on a strong lead but that I'd need some working capital to make sure that I can *continue* working on it."

"And you also said that if you found the killer you wanted ten thousand dollars."

"Why would you object to that? I'm sure you offered Clint Adams a bonus to find the killer."

"Clint Adams is quite a different case."

"How's that?"

"He had a woman friend who was killed by the Ripper. He's also a very busy man—too busy to be doing this for his own gain." Porter looked at Graves as if the small man were little more than a buffalo chip. "You, on the other hand, look very much like a confidence artist."

"I am a journalist," Graves said with all the dignity and pride he could muster.

"A journalist? That's what you call yourself, is it?"

Graves stood up.

"I need five hundred dollars immediately."

The colonel glared at him.

"If I ever find out that this is nothing more than a trick I'll kill you myself, Graves." Porter's tone was menacing. "Is that understood?"

"Well, now—"

The colonel looked over at Ling Chi and asked, "Am I exaggerating, Ling?"

Ling Chi smiled.

"No sir, you are not exaggerating at all. And if you should fail in keeping your promise for some reason I would be honored to carry it out for you."

Graves sensed that the old fear, his cowardice, was coming back at him again—a fear averted only when Colonel Porter laid five hundred dollars on his desk.

"For this, Graves, I expect results."

Less than a minute after Graves left, Porter looked at Ling Chi and asked, "What do you think, Ling?"

"I would not trust him," Ling Chi said, and then added, "not even if he changed his suit."

"I agree."

With that Porter dispatched Ling Chi to find Sheriff Halsey and tell him about the offer Graves had made.

In doing this, Porter simply felt that he was hedging all of his bets. He didn't really care who caught the killer—Clint Adams or the ridiculous little man who had just left—as long as he was caught.

SIXTEEN

Two hours later Clint sat in Sheriff Halsey's office and listened in disbelief.

"Your friend Graves claims to be onto a lead and he promised the colonel he'll be able to produce the killer within forty-eight hours—if the colonel agreed to pay him ten thousand dollars when he does."

"Graves made that arrangement?"

"Yes, Clint, our Rupert Graves. The shabby little man who just four hours ago was going to cooperate and assist us in our investigation."

"He knows something that he's not telling us," Clint said, "maybe something that he saw in that room."

"Then he knows where this mystery man is?"

"I don't know," Clint said, standing up, "but I'm going to find that little man and have a serious talk with him."

• • •

The suit he found was nearly as loud and just as comic as the one he unceremoniously dumped in the haberdasher's trash basket. He did not seem to notice that the haberdasher's employees were watching him make a fool of himself as he strutted back and forth in his new suit, puffing on a huge cigar.

Graves had already spent two hundred dollars of the Colonel's money on clothing. He meant to spend a hundred more this afternoon doing something he'd longed to do since arriving in town: sneak into Selena's.

Graves was still being a peacock when Clint, who had walked through the business district in search of the little man, came through the door.

Clint went right up to Graves and said, "I want to talk to you."

"I'm pretty busy at the moment, Adams. Why not let me buy you a steak dinner tonight at the Eldorado and then we can talk?"

Clint took the little man by the collar and the seat of his pants and said to the haberdasher, "Do you have a back door?"

The haberdasher hastily drew back a curtain and pointed to a back door.

Running Graves ahead of him Clint headed for the back door and outside.

"What the hell do you think you're doing?" Graves demanded. "You'll mess up my new clothes."

"Just what do you think you're doing, Graves?" Clint asked, releasing his hold on the man.

"I don't know what you're talking about," Graves said, puffing on his big cigar arrogantly.

Clint grabbed the stogie from the man's face and threw it to the ground, stomping it out.

"We're trying to find this butcher who likes to carve up women and you're trying to cash in on him."

"Maybe I know something you don't."

"If you do, you owe it to the Sheriff to tell him."

"No, I don't. The only person I owe anything to is myself. Oh, yes, and to you. Here's the money I owe for my rent. The colonel's agreed to——"

"I heard about your deal with Porter, Graves, and I'm not impressed."

"I wish you'd calm down, my good man. I'm merely practicing free enterprise."

Clint pushed Graves up against the wall of the haberdasher's.

"I want you to tell me what you know before somebody else gets killed."

"Get your hands off me!"

Clint shook his head and released Graves. He wasn't much for beating up on smaller men, though he wished now that Graves was larger so he could hit him.

"Thank you," Graves said, adjusting his new suit. "Now, let me tell you this. If I can capture the killer and turn him over——what's the harm if I collect ten thousand dollars?"

Clint said nothing.

"Just because you're high-minded and wouldn't take the colonel's money——"

"Let me ask you something, Graves."

"What?"

"Do you know what you're getting yourself into?"

"What's that supposed to mean?"

"It means that word has gotten around to the killer that you know something about him. It means that the killer is going to come looking for you."

Graves gulped then and sweat suddenly shone on his forehead.

"You're a weak man, Graves, and a frightened one. Greed has blinded you to those facts——but believe me, you've put yourself in a great deal of jeopardy."

"But Adams, listen—"

"Graves, I'm telling you for your own sake, tell me or the sheriff what you know."

For a moment the fear overcame Graves and it looked as though he was going to talk—but then he sighed and said, "Don't you see, Adams, this is the only chance I'll ever get."

"For what?"

"For this kind of money."

"You're a fool, Graves. You know the kind of killer we're dealing with."

"Yes, I know."

"He'll find you and he'll do to you what he's done to those women."

"I could go back to London as a success."

"Yeah, or you could go back in a box."

Graves looked frightened again, but still said nothing.

"All right, Graves, then you're on your own. I'm not going to waste my time with you."

And with that Clint left, going around the alley to the front street.

After a few moments Graves took a deep breath, realized that he hadn't finished shopping and went to the rear door of the shop.

And found it locked.

SEVENTEEN

Marcie Hatter was a weary woman in her mid-thirties. At one time she'd probably been very good-looking but she had caught most of the diseases inherent to her profession and as a result had bad teeth, loose flesh and a cynical eye.

Even a drover who'd been pushing beef for four months would have a hard time working up much enthusiasm over Marcie Hatter.

Jessica had arranged for Marcie to go for a late afternoon stroll along the river.

Clint was waiting there.

After the amenities Clint said, "I understand you knew Sally Raines?"

"Yes. Back in Omaha."

"You worked together?"

She touched her billowy breasts, her best feature.

"Believe it or not it was ten years ago. I was quite a looker, then."

"I'll bet you were."

"They paid a price for me then, you know?"

"You knew Helen, too, one of the other women who was killed?" he asked, ignoring her reminiscences.

"Yes. She was in Omaha, too."

That interested Clint, that all three of them had come from Omaha.

"What about the other victims?"

"What about them?"

"Were they from Omaha, too?"

She smiled toothlessly.

"Sure. Those were the good old days. We was all young and pretty then. I mean, to be honest, I was ten years older than the other girls, but I kept my looks pretty good."

"Didn't you think to tell the sheriff that?"

"What?"

"The fact that you're all from Omaha?"

"What's so special about that?"

"Don't you find that as sort of a coincidence?"

She shrugged.

"No. There's a lot of girls from Omaha."

"You mean here in town?"

"Sure."

"Why is that?"

"Used to be a local house back there that broke their girls in kind of young and shipped them out to different places. I used to teach young girls the tricks myself—that's how I met Helen, and Sally Raines. Broke 'em in, you might say. Then they started helpin' me break in other young girls."

"Can you think of anything else that might help me, Marcie?"

"I just want you to catch him, that's all!"

"Do you have any guess about who I might be looking for?"

"I'm sure you know about the parson."

"Yes."

"Or the sheriff. He used to beat some of us girls up pretty good. Whenever he got drunk and started thinkin' about his wife."

Clint's eyes narrowed. This was the second such reference to the Sheriff that he had heard. He was going to have to check this out.

"Anybody else?"

"Anybody who hates whores—that's a whole lot of people."

"But nobody specific?"

"Huh-uh. Nobody specific."

"I appreciate you talking to me, Marcie."

She stood up, looking old and tired.

"I just want you to catch him."

By dinner time the sun was a streaky blood red behind the mountains. Clint sat at the Eldorado House sipping coffee and eating beef, hash brown potatoes and green beans.

The temperature had dropped fifteen degrees in the last hour. The fog was rolling in.

Clint had the uncomfortable feeling that it was going to be a busy night.

EIGHTEEN

The killer took the knife from the case and stared at it.

With the dying sunlight spilling through the window, the blade of the knife seemed to still be stained blood red, with the blood of its previous victims.

The killer stared out the window, feeling the familiar delicious rush of excitement.

Soon now.

Soon.

NINETEEN

Graves found the railroad men who worked with Gil Evars. They were drinking in a saloon with a player piano that didn't work quite right. It sounded out of tune.

He went up to them standing at the bar and laid a small stack of greenbacks between them.

They looked at each other and then at Graves.

"Help you?" one of them said.

"I understand that a friend of mine took some money belonging to one of you."

"Who might your friend be?"

"Gil Evars."

The first man snorted.

"Crazy Gil? Hell, he didn't take no money. We was just havin' some fun with him. We'll tell the sheriff that we found it and made a mistake and they'll let him out of jail."

The second man laughed.

"Crazy Gil sure did break up the place some, though."

"He gets these fits, you see," the first man said.

"Some say he's possessed."

Graves said, "You see that money?"

"We sure do, Mister."

"I want you to take it."

"For what?"

"For going down to the jail right now and telling the sheriff that you made a mistake and that you think he should let Gil Evars go."

They counted the money.

"That's a lot of money," the first one said.

The second man looked at Graves suspiciously.

"People don't just go around handin' out money like that. What do you want us to do?"

"Gil isn't doing real well in that jail. He needs to be out of there as soon as possible."

Both men finished their beer and slammed the mugs down on the bar.

"We hear you."

"Loud and clear."

Twenty minutes later Graves waited in the shadows around the corner of the jail for Gil Evars to appear.

It was a chilly and foggy night.

Perfect for what Graves had in mind.

At dusk a deputy began patrolling the business district. He tried various doors to make sure they were locked and then passed onto the next one. In the fog and gloom his footsteps on the boardwalk sounded lonely.

Clint, finishing up his meal at the Eldorado, glanced through the window and saw the deputy. After leaving more than enough to pay for his dinner

check, he picked up his hat and hurried out the door
after the man.

Now there were two sets of feet pounding out
lonely rhythms on the boardwalk.

The deputy, suspicious, stopped and turned, trying
to see who was following him.

He ducked into an alley.

In moments, Clint found himself standing in fog
so thick he could hardly see his hand in front of him.

And no sign of the deputy.

Clint wondered what had happened to the man.
He didn't have to wonder long.

"Just hand me your gun and don't say a word until
I tell you."

Clint, knowing better than to trifle with the no-
nonsense voice, handed over his gun.

Gil Evars looked more like a yokel than ever.

Graves watched him from the trees on the side of
the sheriff's office.

Evars scratched his head and seemed about to set
off in one direction when he stopped and scratched
his head again, then seemed ready to start off in the
opposite direction.

Graves smiled to himself, patting the fifth of
whiskey he had in his pocket.

Oh yes, Evars was perfect for what Graves had in
mind.

Evars started away from the jail finally, an awk-
ward, gangling person who was still more boy than
man.

Graves quickly caught up with him.

"Hey, Gil."

"Mr. Graves! You surprised me."

Graves fell into step with Evars.

"I just wanted to make sure that you had been
released."

"It was the darndest thing. Those two men I work with on the railroad? Well, they came and told the sheriff that it had all been a mistake and that I hadn't stolen anything after all, so he let me go."

Graves waited a moment so that his words would have bigger impact.

"I told them to come down to the jail and tell the Sheriff that."

"You did?"

"Yes."

"Well, thank you very much, Mr. Graves. I truly appreciate that. No one has ever done anything like that for me before."

"Since we're friends, Gil, how about calling me Rupert?"

"Well, sure thing, Mr. Graves. Sure thing."

Graves laughed to himself. He couldn't believe his luck in finding Evars even now.

The gods were smiling. Indeed they were.

"Say, you know something, Mr. Graves—I mean, Rupert?"

"What's that?"

"I'm not sure what direction we're headin."

Graves again patted the bottle in his pocket.

"I'll bet you've still got a headache."

"Now that you mention it, Rupert, I kind of do."

"That's from the alcohol."

"Really? I guess you're right," Evars said, rubbing his head. Graves knew that the more he talked about the headache, the worse it would get.

"Well, I'll tell you what the cure for that is," Graves said, patting the young man on the back. "You need some more."

"Oh, no, Mr. Graves—I mean, Rupert,—alcohol is exactly what I don't need."

"That's the only way to cure you, you know. The hair of the dog."

"The hair of the dog?"

"An expression. It means to cure what ails you, you need some of what got you sick in the first place."

"You really think I need alcohol?"

"You certainly do."

"Well, I sure do trust you and all, but I'm not sure about the alcohol. No offense, of course."

"Well, I've got a great spot where we could go to have a few nips."

"Where's that?"

"Oh, let's just say a friend of mine's."

Gil Evars looked around at the foggy business district.

"Looks like most of the places are closed down for the night."

"This is a special place."

"What kind of place?" For the first time, Gil Evars sounded almost suspicious.

"Selena's."

"You mean where all those—sinful—women carry on?"

Graves laughed.

"That's exactly where I mean, son."

TWENTY

"Don't move," the deputy said, moving in on Clint.

He took Clint's weapon and pushed him up against the wall.

"Now, why were you following me?"

"I wanted to ask you some questions."

"You're supposed to be the sheriff's friend," the deputy said. "You got any questions, you ask him. I don't like being trailed through the dark in a fog."

"I couldn't ask the sheriff the questions I need answers to."

"Why not?"

"Because the questions are about him."

Curious in spite of himself the deputy asked, "What do you want to know?"

Clint paused. He knew that he could easily spoil his entire investigation—but only somebody who worked with the sheriff could give him a reliable answer.

"The more I investigate the killings, the more the sheriff's name comes up."

"How do you mean? Not as a suspect?"

"Yes."

"You're crazy."

"I've been told that he's beaten women—prostitutes—from time to time."

For a few minutes the deputy said nothing.

"Is it true?" Clint prompted.

"The sheriff might not be a perfect gentleman all the time, but he sure as hell ain't no Ripper."

"So then he has beaten up prostitutes."

"Once or twice things have gotten a little out of hand, maybe . . ."

"You were there when they did?"

The deputy hesitated, then said, "Yes."

"What happened?"

"He just had a little too much to drink and then said some pretty ugly things to her—well, things kind of got out of hand."

"And you stopped it?"

The deputy stared at Clint, wondering how he could have guessed that.

"Yeah, I guess so."

"Didn't he resent you for that?"

"Now, that's the funny thing," the deputy said, as if it had been bothering him for a long time. "He seemed to be relieved that I did it."

They stood silent for a few moments, and off in the distance a coyote sounded, bleak and lonely.

"He's a good man really, Sheriff Halsey."

"From what I know of him, yes, I'd say he is. That's why these incidents bother me."

"I don't want you giving him no grief," the deputy said, forcefully. "He's had enough grief in his life."

"What kind of grief has he had?"

"That don't make no never mind to you."

"Why not? You said yourself I'm supposed to be a friend of his."

"It doesn't concern you. I've said enough as it is." The deputy handed Clint back his gun. "Besides, I've got rounds to make."

"Are you sure you won't say any more? It could be very helpful."

"I'm real sure, Adams. Real sure."

Then he disappeared into the fog. In moments he was again nothing more than disembodied footsteps.

TWENTY-ONE

Except for a light on the second floor, Selena's was dark when Graves and Gil Evars reached the place.

"Damn," Graves muttered, "Maybe they won't let us in after all."

Evars did not sound unhappy.

"I'm not sure this is a right good idea anyway, Mr. Graves."

"Rupert, my boy, Rupert."

"I mean, I'd sure hate for anybody to find out I'd ever been—well, up there."

Graves slapped Evars manfully on the shoulder.

"Come on, lad. The night's young yet. We'll have a good time, just wait and see."

With that, Graves led the way up the steps. He knocked on the door and waited.

Across the street a curtain fluttered open. A pair of eyes, if they could have been seen, shone like a cat's in the gloom.

• • •

"Why don't you have supper with me?" Colonel Porter asked.

"I'm afraid I've already eaten," Clint Adams said.

"Very well, then," the colonel said, leaning back in the big leather chair in his den. "At least you can share my brandy and have a cigar with me."

A few minutes later, Clint was having a hard time deciding which tasted better—the brandy or the cigar.

"Now, what can I do for you?" Porter asked.

"Two things, actually," Clint said. "First, I'd like to know about the visit you had from Graves."

Porter nodded. All the while savoring his cigar, he told Clint about Graves' visit, ending with, "A distasteful little man."

"Do you really think he knows something?"

"That's the problem with men like Graves—at least in my experience," the colonel said. "You can never be sure about them. Some of them do nothing but daydream all their lives about making the big score—but a few of them actually stumble into something by blind luck."

"So then you don't really have any sense of whether or not he knows something he's not telling us?"

"Afraid I don't." The colonel nodded to the bar behind Clint and asked, "More brandy?"

"No thanks. I've got the feeling I have a long night ahead of me."

The colonel nodded his head in sympathy.

"You did mention two things."

"Before I go on I want to make certain that anything that is said here has no bearing on the sheriff's job."

"Why would it?"

Clint didn't answer.

"All right. You have my word."

"Have you heard any rumors about the sheriff?"

"You hear rumors about everyone at one time or another. What kind of rumors did you have in mind, specifically?"

"That he has beaten up female prisoners. Especially prostitutes."

"Yes, I've heard stories but I always put them down to idle gossip."

Clint looked at the other men steadily.

"Maybe they're not. At least, they're worth checking out."

For the first time the Colonel set his cigar down and regarded Clint seriously.

"You might have a point, Adams," he said, "you just might have a point."

Graves and Gil Evars were in the darkened vestibule of Selena's pleasure house.

"Honey, you mustn't have heard—but the dear parson? Well, he closed us down."

"Officially," Graves said with a wink. "I know you can fix it."

Selena sized him up—which didn't take very long.

Graves heard footsteps pounding down the stairs.

"Selena!"

"What?"

"Jessica's gone!"

"Gone where?"

In the shadows Graves watched as a plump, half-naked whore came breathlessly up to Selena.

"Well, the first thing that happened was that Marcie decided to go for a walk . . . and when she didn't come back right away . . . Jessica went to find her. Now they're both gone!"

"Damn their eyes! They know nobody was supposed to leave this place—not with the Ripper prowling around."

He could see the tears in the whore's eyes.

"I just hope they're all right."

Selena grimaced.

"Yeah, baby, so do I." She kissed the whore on the cheek in a comforting manner, then turned and looked at Graves, who was eyeing the whore's big breasts.

"Well, let's get your young friend taken care of."

TWENTY-TWO

Jessica was lost.

Dante was not so big a town that you could turn a corner and find an area you've never seen before—but in the fog it might well have been Chicago or New York. She could could not figure out where she was.

"Marcie!"

The plaintive sound of her voice reminded her of a time when she was a young girl and had lost her new kitten. It had drifted off on a foggy night like this one and she had searched until her ma and pa had to come looking for both of them. She'd never found her new kitten. She could still remember the ache in her chest for months afterward whenever she thought about the little kitten.

"Marcie!"

But there was no sign of her and that peculiar ache was beginning in Jessica's chest again . . .

• • •

After he left Colonel Porter's Clint started back to town to have a talk with the sheriff. It was pointless to continue this line of investigation behind the sheriff's back—better to confront the man and see how he reacted.

Behind the fog you could smell winter coming down from the mountains for its six month stay.

The days of Indian summer were numbered.

His feet touched wooden boardwalk now as he entered the town proper. He had gone a short distance when he heard the screams. Orienting himself in the fog was difficult. He had to listen again for the next scream before deciding which way to go.

He chose the middle of the street because he was less apt to trip over something like an errant chair or barrel. He took his gun out and moved as quickly as he could.

Another scream.

He moved toward the sound of it as if it were a lighthouse.

She ran into him.

As he moved through the billowing clouds of damp gray gloom, she appeared in a silhouette made by a street lamp. She was still screaming and she ran right into him.

Even before he got full hold of her he felt the blood sopping her right arm. She collapsed into his embrace. He brushed her hair back from her face and marveled again at her beauty. He'd seen very few women the equal of Jessica.

He pulled off his jacket and lowered her to the ground, using the jacket as a pillow for her head. Kneeling beside her he ripped away what was left of her sleeve so he could get a better look at her arm. Using his bandana he fashioned a makeshift torniquet to stem the flow of blood.

Her eyes fluttered open.

"Is Marcie—dead?"

"Where is Marcie?" Clint asked gently.

"I found her . . . we were talking . . . and he . . . jumped out at us . . . from the shadows . . . started . . . stabbing." Jessica was obviously describing an attack by the Ripper.

Footsteps came towards them, running.

"What's going on here?"

The voice was familiar. Sheriff Halsey. "Is she all right?" he asked, crouching down next to Clint.

"She's been stabbed," Clint said. "She says Marcie was hurt, too."

"The Ripper?"

"Sounds like it."

"Damn. Where's Marcie?"

Clint leaned over Jessica, whose eyes were fluttering as she began to focus on Clint's face.

"Jessica, can you take me back to where Marcie is?"

"Over—over by the milliner's, I think."

"I'll go and look," the sheriff said.

Now two other men came running up, one of them the deputy Clint had spoken to earlier.

Clint touched Jessica's hand.

"They'll stay with you, Jessica. I have to go and see if I can help Marcie."

"Help Marcie . . ." she whispered.

"Get her a doctor," Clint said to the deputy, and as he and the sheriff headed for the milliner's, the man with the deputy went for the doctor.

Clint and Halsey set off on the run. The milliner, the sheriff said, was two blocks away.

It took ten minutes to find her and when they did, they almost wished they hadn't.

The sheriff grabbed a kerosene lamp hanging on a

nearby post and brought it over to where she was lying, half in an alley. Like the others she had been disemboweled and her private parts ripped and torn.

"My God," Halsey said.

Clint listened carefully to his voice. Was it the sound of a man faking shock—after he'd done the killing himself?

TWENTY-THREE

The sheriff took Clint to the south end of town, to
the doctor's office. The stone building was a small
hospital, but the only staff was the one doctor, a
small, bewhiskered man in his early sixties who
smelled of alcohol—of both the medicinal and the
recreational variety.

"Sheriff," the doctor greeted, letting them in.

"Seth, did they bring the girl—"

"I was just about to work on her when you
knocked."

The doctor turned and the sheriff and Clint followed. He led them into a room where Jessica was
lying on a table. She was covered to her neck with a
sheet, but her bloody injured arm was exposed. The
table was surrounded by several kerosene lamps.

"And now, if you gentlemen don't mind, I don't
like to operate with an audience."

They waited outside while he worked on Jessica.

* * *

Gil Evars gulped and knew for certain that he had just condemned himself to the fires of hell forever.

He was in a room upstairs at Selena's.

Before him stood a whore named Sadie Lee. She had just unbuttoned her nightgown and let her huge breasts spill free. They danced before him, their silver-dollar-sized nipples winking at him, until he had no choice but to lower his eyes or go crazy.

"I'd have to say that I've never had that particular reaction before," Sadie Lee said, putting her hands on her hips and regarding the young man quizzically.

"These here tits are the biggest and best you're likely to find in Dante. I mean, just in case you don't think they're big enough for you?"

Gil kept his eyes down.

"No, Ma'am, I mean, they're fine, they're... plenty big enough."

"Well then, why don't you come on over here and start suckin' on them, or something. Come on, honey, these tits love being loved."

She cupped them in her hands, thumbing the nipples so that they swelled up before his bulging eyes.

"You're afraid of me, aren't you?" she asked, suddenly.

Evars couldn't find his tongue. His mouth was suddenly very dry, and his penis was swelling rapidly, tightening his pants.

"I said, you're afraid of me, aren't you?"

"Yes, Ma'am."

"I can barely hear you."

"I said... yes."

"You've never done it before, have you?"

"No, Ma'am."

"You want to do it but you're scared to, right?"

"Uh, yes, Ma'am."

She stepped closer to him and he could feel the warmth given off by her big body. He felt his heart beating so hard that he was sure it would rip right through him.

"You want to do it with me, don't you?"

Silence.

"Don't you?"

"Yes, Ma'am."

"Well, then, we'll start off with lesson number one."

When she put her hand down the front of his pants he thought he would lose his mind. With her other hand she unbuttoned his pants and let them drop low enough so that she could fish his cock out of his underwear, where it stood straight and tall.

"Ooh, this is a *nice* one," she said, stroking it slowly. Sadie was almost forty and had been a whore for twenty-five years. This boy was barely twenty and his body was smooth and clean. She was going to enjoy him.

"Why don't I lead you over to the bed?" she said.

And so she did, taking a firm hold on his cock and walking him over to the big, down-filled bed.

"Lie down, honey," she said, pushing him down on the bed. She took off his boots, pulled his pants entirely off and then his underwear. She leaned over him then and surrounded his cock with her big breasts, rolling it between them.

Gil moaned and stared at the ceiling.

She leaned over him further and took his long, smooth cock into her mouth.

"Mmm, baby boy, you are a sweet one," she murmured, licking him up and down like a licorice stick. "Oh, yeah, Momma's gonna treat you real special."

She lowered her mouth over him again, engulfing him and sucking. It was all Gil could take and he exploded like a geyser into her educated mouth.

Gil Evars just knew that he was going straight and forever to the fiery flames of hell!

• • •

Clint stood over Jessica and watched her beautiful face become even more tender as she slept.

The sheriff came up behind him.

"She sure is beautiful."

"Yes."

The doctor poured himself a stiff one.

"One for you?" the doctor asked.

"Thanks," Clint said gratefully.

"Will she be here all night?"

The doctor nodded.

"Whoever put that tourniquet on her arm saved her life—or at least, her arm."

"Well then, that's something to drink to, isn't it?" Clint said.

"Son," the doctor said, "I never need a reason to drink."

Graves stood outside the door where young Gil Evars was having carnal knowledge of a woman for the first time in his life. Graves smiled broadly to himself. He felt like a right nice person, doing that for such a hapless young man.

But of course it was the least he could do, considering the other plans he had for the young man.

A door opened down the hall and a woman stepped out. She was a fleshy woman, too old to be worth much as a whore, but there was an earthy, slutty quality about her that stirred Graves' loins.

"Well, what are you waiting out here for?"

"A friend," he said, pointing to the closed door.

"Aren't you a little lonely out here?" she asked. She opened her robe a bit so he could see her big, heavy breasts. They had begun to sag, but again her body had an earth mother quality.

"A little."

"Like to come in here and . . . wait?"

Graves felt that this was further indication that his luck was changing.

"Why not?"

When Gil Evars came the second time he bellowed. The whore riding him used the opportunity to pour some more whiskey down his throat. His cock was buried in her to the hilt and his hands were squeezing her tits. She'd been paid to feed him as much liquor as possible, but there was nothing said about her not getting some pleasure for herself. The young man's cock had refused to go down after she'd sucked him the first time, and now she was riding him up and down, enjoying the way his stiff young cock poked at her insides.

Evars was babbling beneath her, slurring his words as the liquor continued to take effect.

And then he came, and bellowed . . .

Graves had watched while the heavy whore undressed, his cock stiffening as her naked breasts swayed into view. The nipples were very large and dark as copper. She had a roll of flesh around her belly, but that didn't matter. She came over to him, popped his cock out of his pants and began to suck on it while he played with her big tits.

That was all that mattered.

It was only minutes before Graves was once again standing outside the door of the room where Gil Evars was.

When Graves heard the sounds that Gil was making he was glad that the young man was happy.

After all, he was going to kill him within the hour.

TWENTY-FOUR

After word spread that another harlot had been killed, and a second wounded, Parson Robeson's flock knew enough to head straight for the church, where their spiritual leader awaited them.

"We can no longer permit this!" he shouted, bringing his fist down on the pulpit once.

A man rose. He wore a three-piece suit and his hair and sideburns were cut to a "respectable" length. Seated to his left were his plump wife and three plump children—all very respectable.

"I say," the man shouted, "that we do what the Bible has ordered us to do when sin will not flee from the face of purity and righteousness."

"The purifying fires!" the congregation shouted.

"The fires that cleanse!" shouted the parson. "The fires that destroy Satan himself!"

It was then that the rest of the respectable flock took up their own chants until the air was filled with threats and oaths spoken all together, so that it sounded like one great voice speaking in a foreign language. To be sure, their minds were all filled with the same powerful thoughts.

Eyes bulged, faces filled with blood, spittle showed silver on even the mouths of children.

And all Parson Robeson had to do was lead this tide of human rage out of the church onto the street, pausing only to fill their hands with torches—which the parson just happened to have handy. He had been waiting for the opportunity to turn his flock into an mob angry enough to burn Selena's house to the ground—with the whores inside!

They spilled into the night carrying lighted torches and marched boldly down the street. There were so many torches that their heat almost burned away the fog.

There could be very little doubt as to where they were going.

The saloon buzzed with talk about the latest Ripper killer.

Clint and the sheriff stood listening at the bar, amused and amazed at how the story became distorted and exaggerated as it passed from mouth to mouth.

"I'd like to know where our friend Graves is," Clint said to Halsey.

"So would I."

"Why don't we finish these and go looking for him?" Clint suggested.

Halsey nodded and said, "Good idea. I'm tired of listening to all this crap. This guy at the end of the bar says that the Ripper tore four women apart and nobody can get the right pieces together again."

"Idiots."

They finished their drinks and set the empty glasses down on the bar. As they were about to leave

Halsey froze Clint with his next words.

"I hear you had a talk with one of my deputies about me tonight."

Clint hesitated, looked into the sheriff's eyes and said, "That's right, I did."

"Can't say as I especially appreciate that. Did you have a particular aspect of my life in mind?"

So apparently the deputy had told Halsey about *a* conversation, but no specifics.

"I have to check everything out, sheriff," Clint said. "I'd heard certain . . . rumors about you and wanted to check them out."

"Why didn't you just come to me?"

"I was on my way to talk to you when I heard Jessica screaming."

"Well," Halsey said, "I've got a story to tell, if you're interested in hearing it."

"I sure am."

"Come on," Halsey said, "we can talk on the way."

Gil Evars bayed at the moon as lustily as any hound dog.

Graves thought that it was a good thing he had decided to take the boy down the alleys.

Evars was a wobbly, noisy drunk. He stank of sex and whiskey. He was drunk enough so that he had totally forgotten about the fires of hell.

"I wanna go back for more," he complained to Graves.

"Soon, lad, soon. We just have to take a little walk."

"I want to try one of the other girls," he said as they walked. "I want a younger one, with smaller, uh, tits, and then I want one with different color hair . . ."

"Whatever you want, kid. It's yours."

Slapping Graves on the back Gil said, "You sure are a good ol' frien' of mine, Rupert."

"Thank you, Gil."

"I like you," Gil said, throwing his arm around the smaller man's neck.

"I like you too," Graves said. As he spoke he pulled a gun from his belt.

"Why don't we stop here for a minute and catch our breaths?"

"Sure thing, Mr. Graves—oops, I mean, Rupert."

He was so drunk he didn't see Graves raise the gun and then bring it down on his head. Gil Evars slumped to the ground. Graves put the gun back in his belt, took the boy under the arms and dragged him to their destination, just around the corner. The rooming house where the "stranger" lived, the man no one had ever seen.

All the lights were out in the house, everyone was probably fast asleep. The house was filled either with laborers who were early to bed, or elderly people who retired even earlier.

He dragged Gil Evars around to the back where the rear door posed little problem. He forced the cheap lock and then dragged the unconscious man inside and up the steps to the room on the top floor.

Just outside the room Graves paused, almost losing his nerve. Finally, he forced the door and dragged Gil Evars into the room. He lowered him onto the bed and looked around. He was careful not to make any noise, and used only the light of the moon to see.

The room looked just as he had fixed it up in the first place—just as it had been when he showed it to Clint Adams and Sheriff Halsey. He had painstakingly saved all the newspaper clippings from all over the country, and from Europe, about prostitutes being cut up, and then put them all up on the wall of the room. The room of the Ripper, just as Graves had planned it.

He smiled and took from his pocket a small bottle.

He held it up to the moonlight so he could read the label: CYANIDE, with a little skull and crossbones.

He went over to the bed where Gil Evars slumbered on and knelt beside him, raising the open bottle to the young man's lips.

TWENTY-FIVE

By now the parson's torch-bearing flock ringed Selena's, the flames of their torches dissipating the fog.

From the upstairs window the eleven prostitutes who lived in the house looked down at the mob from their windows, in anger and in fear.

They all turned to Selena, their surrogate mother, for guidance.

"What are they going to do, Selena?" one prostitute asked.

"I'm afraid they're gonna burn us out, honey."

"They're gonna let us out first, ain't they, before they start burning?" another girl asked.

Selena looked grim.

"Let's hope so, honey. Let's hope so."

Somehow, though, she didn't think it was very likely.

• • •

The sheriff's tale was a simple enough one.

Ten years ago his wife died during an outbreak of anthrax. Theirs had been a childless marriage, and the sheriff had taken her death particularly hard. Only after a few years had gone by did he show any interest in women again and the first one he hooked up with turned out to be a bad one.

She was too young for him, and far too wild, but he was in his late forties, lonely and flattered by her attention. He was so flattered that even though it was obvious to everyone else in Dante, Halsey could not see that she was a bodacious flirt and an expert in unfaithfulness.

The sheriff went ahead and married the young woman. On his wedding night he discovered her true nature. She'd drifted off to see a farmhand that she had been seeing on the sly. He saw them in each other's arms in a late summer field and he went berserk. He beat the man badly and forced him to leave town. He also, if not quite as badly, beat his new wife. Up to that point he had never so much as raised his hand to a woman, and he became ashamed of himself. Two days later he gave her all the money in his savings account, took her to the train depot and bade her goodbye.

"It was like a sickness," Halsey told Clint. "Three times afterward I got very drunk and felt I was in a strange mood. I made the mistake of going down to the jail to check things out—and I saw the prostitutes. In my drunken state all I could see was my second wife, so I beat each of them in turn." He sighed and said, "I haven't done anything like that in four years, now."

Clint nodded grimly. It was not hard to see the shame in the sheriff's eyes.

Halsey's hand trembled as he rubbed his face.

"But I'm not the Ripper," he finished.

"No," Clint said, "I don't believe you are."

Halsey looked at Clint and said, "Thanks, Adams."

"Well . . . thanks for being frank with me. I know it couldn't have been easy to tell me all of that . . . and call me Clint."

"All right, Clint."

They were walking down the street when suddenly someone came running out of the fog and ran into them.

"Charlie," the sheriff said, catching the man.

"Oh, Sheriff, I was coming to find you. The parson and his people, they're burning down Selena's!"

For a moment Graves sensed that Evars was going to awaken as the cyanide was taking effect.

In the darkened room Evars began to claw at the air and jerk about the way men do when they are hanged.

Once, his eyes fluttered open.

Graves stared down at the young man, almost feeling sympathy for him. Graves had nothing against the kid personally. It was just that he was the perfect patsy to help Graves take advantage of the one opportunity he had for real money in his forty years of living.

A few minutes later Evars started frothing at the mouth. Silver bubbles formed around the edges. Choking sounds came from his throat. Graves smiled to himself. It was going to work.

Clint and Sheriff Halsey reached Selena's just as one of the mob threw a rock through the window. By the time Clint came abreast of the crowd he had the safety off the Winchester he'd picked up at Halsey's office on the way. The sheriff held a similar weapon.

Clint and Halsey positioned themselves on Selena's porch and pointed the rifles at the crowd.

"Robeson, tell them all to go home before some-body gets hurt," Halsey said.

But the parson wasn't intimidated by the rifles.

"If we did not have whores in our midst, then our streets would be safe for women and children to walk. You have brought the curse of Our Lord down on us by letting them operate here."

By the end of his little speech the parson's hands were flailing at the air and his long white hair was flowing in the breeze.

"We're going to drive them out ourselves, since you won't do it, Sheriff," somebody from the mob said.

"Nobody's driving anybody out," Halsey shouted. "The first man who throws a torch gets a bullet."

"He's bluffing," the parson told his flock.

Clint looked over at Halsey and could see that he was bluffing, all right. He wasn't prepared to shoot any of the townspeople.

"We must burn them out," Parson Robeson shouted, and the mob started coming closer.

Clint fired a shot in the air and they stopped.

"Move away from the parson," he shouted.

Slowly, the mob dispersed so that there was no one around the parson.

"Now you're the one who is going to get a bullet, Parson, if this crowd doesn't go home."

The crowd waited tensely to see what the Parson would do next.

"He's bluffing!" he shouted, raising his arms over his head, his hands closed into fists. "Follow me and we will smite the whores of Babylon."

Clint knew that they had to convince this crowd they meant business. He also knew that the Sheriff was not going to do it.

As the crows began to close in again Clint said,

"Shit," and shot Parson Robeson in the left arm, above the bicep.

The parson wheeled, cried out and grabbed his arm, and fell heavily to his knees.

"Now go on home," he said to the shocked crowd.

They would have gone home, too, had not someone yelled, "Look, the house is burning."

Clint and Halsey turned and could see that smoke was filling the house.

"Somebody got around behind us and tossed in a torch," Halsey said. "This old house will go up like a tinder box."

He jumped down from the porch and grabbed a man from the mob.

"Go and tell the fire volunteers to bring their water and hoses down here fast!"

"I won't do anything to help the whores—" the man started to protest, but Halsey slapped him hard.

"If they're not here in five minutes I'm going to hold you personally responsible. Now move!"

The man took off down the street.

"The rest of you get some buckets. We're going to form a bucket brigade."

The sheriff turned to say something to Clint, but he wasn't there.

The Gunsmith had run into the burning house.

Jessica woke from one nightmare to another.

The hospital room was small and dark. Shadows from the corridor outside played like phantoms on the wall.

Now there was noise, too, from outside. She could hear the fire brigade rushing by.

She could sit up just enough to see the distant flames at the other end of town licking at the black sky.

Her strength left her then and she had to lie back

on the pillows. Her arm began to throb again.

The had given her morphine and she was still groggy. She tried to close her eyes when an image from earlier in the evening sprang unbidden to her mind.

The image was of Marcie being stabbed . . . again . . . and again . . . and again . . .

Jessica screamed.

TWENTY-SIX

Clint found a door on the side of the house and smashed it open with his heel.

Covering his head with his jacket he ran into the hall and found the stairway. From the top, billowing smoke began to descend, and he could hear the screams.

The flames had not yet reached this part of the house but thick, deadly smoke had filled the upper hall.

He started up the steps. He could hear the women panicking and he knew he was going to have to go up after them.

He went up and when he reached the hall called out to anyone who could hear him.

"Over here!"

Tongues of flames lapped at the walls, lighting the hall. The women ran from where they had been cowering and stood on the other side of the flame.

"You'll have to run through it," he called out.

"Wait until I tell you."

He found a doorway, ran in and pulled a blanket off a bed. He carried it out to the hall and then called out to the women.

"One at a time. Come on!"

If any of their clothes or hair had caught fire as they ran through he smothered it with the blanket. The last woman through was Selena, whose hair had caught fire. Clint smothered it before she could be seriously injured.

"Is everyone accounted for?" he asked.

Selena turned and spoke to one of the other girls, then turned back with a worried look.

"Sophia," she said. "Sophia isn't here."

"She must still be on the other side somewhere," Clint said. "I'll have to go and get her."

He wrapped himself in the blanket and ran through the flames. They licked at his heels and his exposed flesh, and then he was through.

"Sophia!" he shouted.

He checked two rooms before he found her, cowering on the floor, covering her head with her hands.

"Come on," he said, grabbing her and pulling her to her feet.

"The photograph," she said.

"Forget it—"

"The photograph," she said, again, "the Ripper..."

He looked on the floor and saw a photograph that was half eaten by the flames. He stepped on it to extinguish it and then picked it up and put it in his pocket.

"The Ripper," she said, again, "photograph."

The implication was clear enough. The photograph had something to do with the Ripper, but he couldn't look at it now. He took her out into the hall. As he wrapped her in the blanket to run through the

flame she suddenly went limp. He had no choice but
to lift her and carry her through. On the other side
Selena asked if she was all right. Clint simply told
her to get out of there.

Seconds later he was standing outside with the
women, the damp air cooling his face. Jeers went up
from the crowd because all of the whores had gotten
out alive—almost.

When Clint put Sophia down and unwrapped the
blanket it was plain from her ashen features that she
was dead. He checked for a pulse anyway but she
was gone.

Two young women standing above him began to
cry. Selena put her arms around them in an attempt to
comfort them.

Guiltily, all Clint could think about was the half-
burned photograph in his pocket, and what it might
mean.

Graves took a surgical knife from his pocket and
placed it on the table next to the bed. Next he took
out a vial of blood from his other pocket, uncapped it
and poured some of it on the knife. The rest he
smeared onto Gil Evars' shirt and right arm. He then
made the right arm dangle to the floor and put the
surgical knife by the hand.

When he was finished he crept to the door,
checked to make sure the hallway was empty, and
then got out of there.

By dawn he'd have the colonel's money and be on
his way out of town—long before anybody figured
out what happened.

TWENTY-SEVEN

"This is an outrage!" Parson Robeson cried from behind the bars of the cell Halsey had put him in. They had allowed the doctor to bandage his arm first. "This gunman shoots me without provocation and you put me in jail!"

"This man," Halsey said (they were both talking about Clint) "was acting as my deputy. You incited that mob to riot, Parson, and to burn that house down, and a woman died as a result."

Robeson snorted and said, "A whore! Surely you can't be arresting me because a whore—"

"A woman died, Parson!" Clint Adams snapped. "That doesn't mean anything to you, does it?"

"A decent woman, yes, but a whore! I have better things to do than mourn a whore!"

"Well then, mourn yourself, Parson," Clint said, "because this was murder, and you're going to hang."

"You can't—"

"Shut up!"

Half an hour later Clint—fresh from a bath—and Sheriff Halsey were in the sheriff's office having coffee. Clint was about to pull the photograph out of his pocket when the office door opened and Colonel Porter's manservant, Ling Chi, entered.

"Ling Chi," Halsey said.

The Oriental executed a slight bow.

"What can I do for you?"

Ling Chi frowned.

"A most peculiar meeting is taking place and I need your advice."

"Sure," the sheriff said.

"Colonel Porter is about to pay that reporter, Graves, the money he asked for."

"Isn't the money for finding the killer?" Halsey asked.

"Graves claims he has."

"What?" Halsey said, standing up.

"Yes. He says he knows who the killer is and will tell the colonel—after he gets his money."

Halsey glanced at Clint.

"I guess we'd better get over there."

"I guess so."

A word burned in her brain.

Omaha.

All of these murders were happening because of something that took place in Omaha.

Just then a woman that the doctor had hired as a temporary nurse walked in.

"The fire wagon woke you up, huh?"

Jessica nodded and whispered, "Yes."

The nurse nodded, then laughed.

"Well, I suppose in your line of work you get used

to spending some pretty restless nights, huh?" She cackled at her own joke and left.

Such treatment did not bother Jessica anymore. As a whore she expected no less.

TWENTY-EIGHT

When Clint, Halsey and Ling Chi arrived at Colonel Porter's they found the house lit up as if for a party.

Ling Chi led them through a side entrance and directly to Colonel Porter's den.

The first thing Clint saw when he entered was Colonel Porter's back. He was standing behind his desk at a wall safe, taking out small packets of greenbacks wrapped in rubber bands.

The next thing Clint noticed was Rupert Graves.

Clint couldn't believe the change that had come over the man since they had met. When he had paid the little man's rent and bought him a meal he had come to the conclusion that Graves was one of those big talking harmless little people. He no longer held that opinion.

Graves did not see Clint right away. He was too busy staring at the money on the desk. When he did look away and spot Clint Adams, he frowned.

"What are you doing here, Adams?"

"Trying to stop you from robbing Colonel Porter, Graves."

"This is none of your business," Graves said.

"I say it is."

The colonel closed the safe and turned around to face the room.

"I'll have to agree with Graves on this, Adams. It's none of your affair."

"Well, it's my affair," Sheriff Halsey said. "Colonel, am I to understand that you're paying Graves because he's found the killer?"

"Yes."

"Then it's his duty to report that fact to the law— namely me."

Graves smiled mockingly.

"I report it to the law I get nothing. If I report it to the colonel I get my money, and he reports it to the law. Who gets hurt?"

Halsey ignored Graves.

"Do you really believe he knows where the killer is?"

"Yes, I do."

Before anyone could speak Sheriff Halsey drew his gun and pointed it at Graves.

"In that case, you're under arrest for withholding information from the law."

Graves looked to the colonel for help and the look on the little man's face said he knew that he was going to get it.

"Halsey," Colonel Porter said, "don't forget who owns this town."

"I'm not forgetting," Halsey said. "I'm also remembering that you said you wanted an honest lawman in this town."

"That's right, I did say that." The colonel calmed down. "Look, I have an idea."

"I'm listening."

"Why don't we all accompany Mr. Graves to where he says the killer is. I'm sure no one can have any objection to that."

"Guess there's no harm in that. How about you, Clint?" Halsey asked.

"I've got no objection. I do have a suggestion, however."

"What's that?"

"Colonel, I suggest you don't give Graves his money until you actually see the killer."

"That makes sense," Porter said, but Clint could see how much his suggestion had displeased Graves.

Good.

The smoke from the fire had permeated the entire town now, and the streets reeked.

Clint, Halsey, Graves and Colonel Porter reached the boardinghouse where Clint and Graves had been the day before, looking for the man called Carver.

"You're saying he's in there?" Clint asked.

"I'm saying there's a good possibility," Graves said. His eyes were on the small suitcase that the colonel was carrying, which held "his" money.

"Just sitting there waiting for us even though he knows we were here yesterday looking for him. Not very smart for a clever killer, wouldn't you say, Colonel?"

"Wait and see, Adams," Graves said, "Wait and see."

With that Graves led the way to the front door and was pounding on it when the others caught up to him.

The frazzled landlady answered the door carrying a kerosene lamp.

"What's going on? We don't rent rooms this late at night."

"Ma'am, do you remember me?" Graves asked.

The woman squinted at him and then said, "Well, yes, I do, You were here yesterday with that gentleman over there." She was pointing to Clint.

"That's right. Now I'm here with Colonel Porter."

"Colonel Porter!" The woman suddenly sounded very nervous. Why was the most important man in town coming to her boarding house?

"Yes, Ma'am, and Sheriff Halsey."

"Well, my goodness, does this have to do with Mr. Carver's room?"

"Yes, Ma'am," Graves said. "We'd like to take another look at it."

"Well, all right, but please try not to wake the other boarders."

"We'll be very quiet, Ma'am," Graves promised, and added to himself—for himself—again.

They went upstairs.

Parson Robeson engaged the deputy assigned to guard him in conversation so the man would not notice what was happening behind him.

A parishioner the size of a circus strongman was sneaking up to the deputy, and when he got within arm's reach looped one massive forearm around the lawman's neck . . . and proceeded to squeeze.

"Don't kill him," the parson hissed.

The parishioner kept the pressure on until the deputy went limp, then dropped him to the floor and took his keys to let the parson out.

"This is against the law, you know," the parson said.

"We need you to lead us, Parson."

"Very well. We will have to get organized. Where is Mr. Jordan?"

"Waiting for us outside."

"And what has happened to all the whores?"

"They split them up and put them in several of the hotels and boarding houses . . . but I learned something interesting."

"What?"

"A friend who works sometimes as a nurse for the doc told me that there's a whore in the hospital—the one that got cut up when the other one got killed."

The parson's eyes blazed. Ideas were already forming in his brain.

"Well then, I'd say we have a hospital visit to make, brother."

"Yes, Parson," the man said, "I'd say we do."

TWENTY-NINE

Even before they opened the door Clint could smell the blood.

"I wonder if I may borrow your lantern?" he asked the landlady.

"Of course."

She handed the lantern over and Clint led the way into the room.

When he was no more than three steps into the room he saw the man on the bed, covered with blood. On the floor he saw the knife by the man's hand, also covered with blood.

All very damning.

Very convenient.

And very damned phony looking.

"There he is, gentlemen," Graves announced dramatically, "there is your Ripper."

They all approached the bed, and it was Halsey who found the note. He read it and passed it to Clint, who read it three times over.

I CAN NO LONGER LIVE WITH MYSELF
FOR WHAT I'VE DONE TO THOSE SCARLET
WOMEN. EVEN THOUGH THEY WERE
WHORES AND SINNERS, I SHOULD NOT HAVE
KILLED THEM. NOW I AM A SINNER, AND I
MUST DIE.

GIL EVARS, THE RIPPER.

"Seems like we've got our man," Colonel Porter
said.

"Yes, it does," Halsey agreed.

"I don't agree," Clint said, and they all looked at
him.

"What do you mean?" Halsey said.

"He's just jealous because he didn't find the killer
first," Graves said.

"What *do* you mean, Adams?" the colonel asked.

"What if somebody killed Evars, smeared him
with blood, forged the note and made it look like he
was the Ripper."

"Why would anybody do that?" the colonel asked.

"For a lot of money."

"What are you implying?" Graves demanded.

"I'm not implying anything, Graves. I'm suggest-
ing that you killed this poor bastard, dragged him up
here somehow, all so you could blame him for the
murders and take your money from the Colonel."

Porter said, "I'm afraid I can't agree with that,
Adams. This man has done just what he promised to
do, lead us to the killer. There's a knife that's probably the murder weapon, there's a suicide note, and
there's all of this blood. What more could you ask
for?"

"Colonel, I think he's been setting this up all
along," Clint said. "Graves rented this room several
months back under an assumed name when he heard
about the murders. He figured he could come here
with his Ripper stories, find some poor slob to pin it

all on, and make a lot of money."

"Certainly you're not saying that Graves is the killer, then?"

"Of Gil Evars, he is."

"But not the whores?"

"No."

"Then who is?"

Clint hesitated because he knew his answer was going to damage his argument.

"I'm not sure."

"Well, if you can't offer a viable alternative, Adams, I've no choice but to accept this man as the Ripper, and pay Graves his money. Perhaps he's right, perhaps you are a little jealous that he found the murderer—although I wouldn't have expected it of you."

"All right," Clint said, "all right, pay him the money, but don't let him leave town."

"What?" Graves asked.

"Why, were you planning on leaving town immediately with the colonel's money?" Clint asked.

"Of course not," Graves lied. That had been exactly what he was planning, and now he was going to have to change plans.

"Then there's no harm in staying a few more days, until we have the killer dead and buried."

Graves could feel Porter's and Halsey's eyes on him, ready to evaluate his reply.

"All right," he said, "I'll stay. I'm not in a hurry to go anywhere. Now may I have my money?"

Porter looked at the case in his hand, and then passed it over to Graves.

"I don't know how you did it, Graves, but I guess you earned it."

Just like everything else he'd heard in the room, Clint didn't agree with that, either.

The sheriff said he was going to go down to the

undertaker's to get him to bring a wagon to pick up the body, and Clint decided to walk with him.

"You really don't believe him, do you?" Halsey said.

"No."

"And you meant everything you said up there?"

"Yes."

"Then you're saying that Graves killed an innocent man just to set him up."

"That's right, and I think Porter is accepting the easy way out of this. He just wants people to think you've caught the Ripper so he can save his mines."

"You can't blame him for that."

"Burt, there's still a vicious killer loose in this town."

"Well, unless you produce him, I'm going to have to accept Gil Evars as the Ripper, and I'm the one who let him out of jail to kill his last girl."

"All the more reason you should be interested in helping me prove that he was not the Ripper."

THIRTY

"What are you doing?"

"Just keep your hands up."

"Oh, my God."

"If you just keep calm nothing's going to happen to you."

"What do you want?"

"You'll see soon enough."

And with that the parishioner struck the nurse on the back of the head, knocking her unconscious. She was not the nurse who had told him about the whore, or they wouldn't have needed to do this.

They had come up from behind her and put a gun to her back. She had frozen immediately.

They began to search and eventually found the room where the whore was.

Even in the dimness of the room Robeson could see who the whore was.

Jessica.

He had seen her walking around town and he had sinned in his heart.

Many times.

He went over to her now and leaned close to her. Her scent was troubling, and he inhaled it deeply. His man Jordan was standing right behind him.

"God, she's beautiful," Jordan said.

"Quiet," Robeson said. Leaning close to Jessica's ear he said, "We need you to come with us."

She woke, startled and afraid, even more lovely now that her eyes were open.

"What's wrong?" she asked.

He could clearly see her marvelous breasts outlined against the thin fabric of her gown.

"You'll be fine, my child. You're going with us."

Fear made her huge gray eyes even larger.

"But why? Where?"

"We will explain in time."

They helped her off the bed and she almost fell. She was still weak from loss of blood.

"We have to hurry," the Parson said, taking her by the other arm and leading her away.

Graves looked at the greenbacks in the suitcase in disbelief, and then closed it. It was almost like a dream. He half expected someone to snatch it away from him.

He and the colonel left the boardinghouse together, after the undertaker, the sheriff and Clint Adams arrived to pick up the body.

The colonel put a cigar in his mouth and wet it before lighting it.

"I trust you are going to use that money wisely," he said to Graves. "It could set you up for life, if you invest it properly."

"Don't you worry about me," Graves said, patting the side of the suitcase. "The first thing I'm going to do is go to California and enjoy the sun for a long time. Maybe have me a woman or two."

The Colonel shook his head.

"In other words, you're going to squander it. Just what I would expect from a man like you."

"What do you mean, 'a man like me'? I found your killer for you, didn't I?"

"Even if you did, that doesn't change the fact that you are a seedy little opportunist too stupid to realize the one good thing that's happened to you in your life."

"I don't have to listen to that kind of talk, not even from you, Colonel—and I don't think I've done too badly."

"Fine, fine. Enjoy your money your way, Mr. Graves—while you have it."

"I intend to do just that!"

Clint said, "You're positive you never saw the man before."

They were in the vestibule of the building where Gil Evars had been found and before the undertaker took the body away Clint asked the landlady if she had ever seen him.

"No, sir, I never saw that man before."

"Take another look, please. Are you sure?"

He pulled the blanket back that had been covering the body and she glanced quickly at the face.

"I'm positive."

"But you did say yesterday that you had seen your mysterious roomer once, didn't you?"

"Yes, sir."

"Would you tell me again what he looked like."

"Well, he wore a dark hat pulled low over his eyes, for one thing, and a kind of cape thrown over his body. To be honest I really didn't get that good a look at him, I'm afraid."

"Do you remember Rupert Graves from yesterday?"

"Of course,"

"Would you say that he might fit the description of the mysterious boarder?"

"Why," she said, thinking back, "yes, I suppose he might. With that cape it was very hard to tell much about him."

"All right, thank you."

They left, Clint and the sheriff following the men from the undertaker's and watching as they loaded the body aboard their wagon.

It was getting on toward dawn now, and the fog was beginning to dissipate. But there was still a chill in the air. Up in the mountains a whistle blew, signalling the start of the day in the mines.

"So you're still saying that Graves planned this out all along," the sheriff said.

"And very carefully."

"But Colonel Porter believes otherwise."

"Colonel Porter believes what he wants to believe, that the Ripper is dead and soon to be buried."

"There isn't a whole lot of evidence to dispute that, Clint."

"I know. I guess I'll just have to get some."

"From where?"

"From the only live witness we have that's seen the Ripper."

"Jessica."

"Right."

"Just then a deputy came running up, breathing heavily from the run.

"Sheriff—"

"What?"

"The parson's been set free."

"How in blazes—"

"Somebody knocked Dooley over the head from behind."

"That's just fine. Now we've got that fanatic running around loose, again."

"And that's not all," the deputy said.

"What now?"

"That whore, Jessica, who was in the hospital?"

"Was?" Clint asked.

"That's right," the deputy said, "she's missing. Either she's been taken, or she just walked out."

She was tied to a chair in a dark room. They had ripped her clothes off, saying something about how she had to be naked to become pure, leaving her nude but for the bandage around her arm.

She had no idea how long she had been there, nor how long she would be.

She wondered if they planned to kill her.

Even though the knife wound hurt, even though they had not been particularly gentle when bringing her here, she still felt alert and reasonably strong.

Strong enough to start working against the ropes that bound her.

She was concentrating on the ropes when the door opened. A narrow strip of golden light angled across the floor. Widening, it fell across Jessica, too, exposing the reddish thatch between her long legs, and one of her beautiful breasts.

"Well, lookie here," a man said, entering, grinning. "Lookie, lookie here."

THIRTY-ONE

"How long ago did this happen?" Sheriff Halsey asked the deputy who had been knocked out.

"Hour, hour and a half, I guess. I musta been out for a while."

The deputy touched his throat, rubbing it.

"You'd better lie down," Halsey said. "We'll get the doc over here to look at you."

The deputy nodded gratefully.

"You didn't get a look at him, huh?"

"No," the deputy said, "I only felt him. God, but he was strong. I thought he was going to choke the life out of me."

"You don't remember him saying anything?"

"No. I think I heard the parson say, 'Don't kill him,' but I ain't sure."

"All right, go on back and lie down. We'll take things from here."

"Thanks, Sheriff."

When the man had gone to lie down the sheriff

said to Clint. "Why don't we grab ourselves some rifles, then we'll go call on the parson."

"He'll be hiding out."

"No, he won't," Halsey said. "He thinks he's above the law. He'll be at his church or at home."

The parson looked at the six men gathered around the table and said, "You know what I'm asking you men to do."

Grimly, they looked at each other and then back to the parson.

"I'm asking you to do something that could very well lead to imprisonment—to the imprisonment of all of us."

One of the men, a merchant, spoke up.

"Speaking only for myself, parson, I'm all for your idea. It's one good way to put the colonel and the sheriff on notice that we want a clean town, and not one with prostitution running rampant."

"I thank you for your support, brother."

"I'm not afraid, either," another man, also a merchant, spoke up. "I'm glad you seized the girl and I'm glad we're going to do what you've got in mind. It's a bold plan, Parson, worthy of Joshua himself."

"Lord love you, brother."

"The only thing I disagree with is the time," a third man said. "I say don't give the sheriff any more time than need be to get out of here. If we're going to do 'er, let's do 'er right now."

Two other men seconded that motion.

They were going on with their debate when they heard the scream from upstairs.

The men looked at each other fearfully.

The parson said, "I will see what's happened."

Even though he was tired from his long night he moved quickly. He was afraid that something might have spoiled his plans. Why would the girl scream?

He climbed the stairs, went down the hallway to where he was keeping her, and flung the door open.

What he saw disgusted him.

There was Frank Ryan, a member of the parson's own flock—a family man—with his pants unbuttoned and his rampant . . . *thing* exposed. He was actually waving it in the face of the evil whore!

When Ryan saw the parson his member shriveled and he started to step backwards.

"You must do penance for this, brother Ryan."

Shamefully, Ryan said, "I know, Parson, I'm sorry, but she . . . she bewitched me. I had no will-power of my own. The devil—"

"Yes, brother, Satan is in this room," Robeson said, approaching the man and placing a hand on his shoulder, "but we will fight him together. You go home to your wife and children now."

"Yes, sir."

"And pray, brother Ryan, as I will pray for your immortal soul."

"Yes, Parson."

Ryan almost bowed before leaving the room, closing the door behind him, leaving the parson alone in the room with the beautiful, naked whore.

"See, whore of Babylon, how you corrupt honest, God-fearing men?"

"I didn't do anything to corrupt him, Parson."

"You exist, woman. You . . . *are* the Devil's own work. No mere mortal woman could be as . . . as beautiful as you are."

Jessica thought that the parson was looking at her kind of funny. There was a strange light in his eyes.

He was staring at her breasts, and then abruptly pulled his eyes away and fixed them on her bandaged arm.

"The Ripper did that?"

"Yes."

"I understand they caught him."

He was not prepared for the shock on her face. He had expected pleasure, relief that the fiend had been caught, but shock—no, that was totally unexpected.

"You are not happy that he was caught?"

"Of course I am."

"You don't seem very happy."

"The wound—then being taken from the hospital and stripped naked—I'm cold, and exhausted."

"You must remain naked, it is the only way you can be truly cleansed."

"Cleansed of what?"

"Of your sin, child, of your sin."

The parson moved closer, until he could feel the heat of her body.

"I want you to know that I hold nothing against you, personally. It is what you represent that I oppose."

"Then you're going to let me go?"

"We need you for something."

"What?"

"I'm not going to tell you right away." He could see he was frightening her. "I am going to pray for you."

"I'd rather you just let me go."

"So you can go right back to your sinful life? No, I can't do that. Not right now."

"But you will let me go at some point?"

"Of course . . ."

Their eyes locked. She saw that the parson's hands were trembling as he studied her breasts and licked his lips.

"There is something strange about you."

"What do you mean?"

"In my time I have ministered to prostitutes and I've found most of them to be very coarse women. You seem to be . . . gentle, graceful, well spoken."

"Thank you, Parson," Jessica said sarcastically.

"It is almost as if you were not a prostitute, at all."

For a moment she thought he was going to touch her.

"I'm just a whore, Parson."

He pulled his hand back as if it had been burned.

"Yes," he said, "yes, you are."

And then he was gone.

THIRTY-TWO

Graves had never been able to hold his liquor well and this morning was no exception. He sat at a table in Eldorado, finishing a big breakfast, and drinking rye one shot after another. His head was already buzzing but he didn't care. He was celebrating.

He was about to have another shot—his tenth?—when he spotted Clint Adams and the sheriff starting up the main street. It was light now and the fog had totally dissipated. Both men carried rifles and they looked angry.

Graves' reporter's instinct took over then. He wanted to know all five W's: who, what, where, when and why. In other words, what the hell was going on?

He stood up unsteadily from the table, took one of Colonel Porter's greenbacks from the moneybelt he had bought and threw it down. He headed for the street.

"Hey, Adams," he called, trotting to catch up, "what's going on?"

Adams turned around and glared at the little man. He had taken an intense dislike to Graves.

"You've got your money, Graves," he said. "Now kindly leave me alone."

Graves appealed to the sheriff.

"Where are you headed, Sheriff?"

"You heard the man, Graves. You've got ·your money, now get away from us."

They kept on walking and Graves fell in behind them.

"I may be a rich man now, but I still got my reporter's nose for news. You fellas are off to somewhere in a hurry, and you're mad."

"And getting madder," Clint said.

Graves took the hint, but didn't back off completely. He went into an alley to a street that paralleled the main street and followed them that way.

When Clint and the sheriff reached the parson's church they stopped.

Graves hid in a nearby hedge to see what was going on.

In the basement of the parson's house the men had already prepared the tar.

It boiled blackly, like a witches' brew in a wide copper pot.

They'd gotten feathers from a chicken coop on a farm outside of town. The farmer was also one of Parson Robeson's flock.

None of the men present had ever done this before, so they were not exactly sure how to proceed. It sounded simple enough, tarring and feathering a person, but when you came right down to it, it was sort of complicated.

The tar bubbling away, one of the men said, "Why don't we tell the parson we're ready?"

One of the other men said, "I feel sort of funny."

"What do you mean?" a third man asked.

"I don't know," the first man said, "I feel kind of . . . excited."

"I know what you mean," another man said, "but it seems a shame to tar and feather a woman who looks like Jessica."

"Ony way we're gonna get rid of prostitution in this town. That's's what your wife wants, isn't it?"

"Sure, same as yours."

"Still, it is Jessica. Maybe we could . . ."

"Why don't we just go and get the parson?" the first man said, interrupting the conversation before it went too far.

Graves went around to the back of the parsonage. Obviously there was something the sheriff and Adams wanted here. He wondered what it was.

He saw that the door was open in back of the place and he could not resist his curiosity.

He went in the back door and up the back steps. He was just drunk enough that the whole thing seemed like a lark to him.

"The parson and his people could be armed," the sheriff said.

"Yeah, they could."

"Meaning you're not scared?"

"Meaning I know this Jessica, Sheriff. She and the other whores have suffered enough." Clint could not forget the way Sally Raines looked after she'd been hacked up.

They stopped in front of the parson's house, within sight of the church.

"I'm going to the door, Clint. Why don't you cover me?"

Clint nodded.

Graves had no idea where he was. He was just following the stairs.

Soon enough he found himself on the second floor, going down a long hallway.

He passed several doors, peeking in and finding nothing.

Far below him he thought he could hear voices.

He opened still more doors, finding nothing. What he found behind the door after that startled him.

He opened it and saw Jessica, the most beautiful of Dante's whores, tied to a chair, completely naked.

First he had come into all of this money that was around his waist—and now a prostitute who made him drool, all trussed up for him, nice and neat.

Rupert Graves' luck was getting one hell of a lot better in a hurry.

Graves went into the room and shut the door behind him.

THIRTY-THREE

Clint cocked the rifle as soon as the front door opened up.

Parson Robeson appeared in the doorway.

"I do not belong in your jail, Sheriff."

Halsey stayed calm.

"Well, I'm afraid that's not something for you to decide, Parson. And once you're in there, for whatever reason, it's against the law to get out without me letting you out."

"I have taken the whore named Jessica."

"Why?"

"I intend to make an example of her."

"You've lost your mind, Parson."

"And you, sir, have lost your soul."

Clint was close enough to hear the conversation, and he had to agree with the sheriff. The parson seemed to have allowed his religious fervor to take him over the edge.

Clint mounted the steps, holding the rifle steady in both hands.

Robeson pointed at him imperiously and said, "If you harm me the whore will be harmed. That is a promise."

"What do you plan to do with her?"

"You don't really expect me to tell you that, do you?"

"Parson," Halsey said sadly. "Why don't you calm down? Maybe I was a little hasty in jailing you. Maybe you didn't order anyone to burn down Selena's. Maybe that person operated on their own."

"I must be going now."

"Don't get yourself in deeper, Parson. Don't make the situation worse."

"I appreciate your advice, Sheriff. I really do."

With that he closed the door. They could hear his footsteps retreating into the house.

"I'm afraid the parson's gone round the bend," the sheriff said.

Clint nodded.

"I want to get Jessica out of there. She doesn't deserve this."

"What do you suggest?"

"I'm going in to get her."

"How can you be sure she's in there?"

"Where else would he put her?"

"In the church?"

"Then he'd be over there and not here. I'm going in, Sheriff."

"How?"

"There must be a back door."

"What would you like me to do?"

"Just what I did for you."

"Cover you?"

Clint nodded.

"All right."

They walked around the house to the back and not only found a back door, but found it open. There was a burning odor in the air that Clint couldn't place.

"You smell that?" he asked.

The sheriff sniffed the air and said, "I smell it. What is it?"

"I don't know, but whatever it is it smells vile."

"Wait a minute," Halsey said, sniffing the air again. "I've smelled that before, when I was down south."

"What is it?"

Halsey sniffed the air again, closed his eyes, and then opened them.

"Tar!"

"What?"

"Burning tar, they're melting tar."

"For what?"

"In the south they use it with feathers . . ."

"Jesus," Clint said. "Cover me."

Five minutes before Clint went through the back door, Graves had come out the back door—with Jessica. He had found her clothes, allowed her to dress, and then taken her out.

She was his, now.

He took her to a rundown saloon where he had done some drinking earlier during his stay in town, and paid the man from his moneybelt for a back room and some privacy.

"You got 'er," the man said, stowing away the money.

Now that they were in the back room Graves nodded to the cot and said, "Take off your clothes. I'll make it worth your while."

Then he went to the window and drew the curtains.

Behind him Jessica said, "I'd really rather not do this."

She was lying on the cot and had not yet removed

her clothing. Her face was pale.

Graves laughed.

"What would have happened if I hadn't take you away from the parson's—care to think about that?"

"I'm grateful, believe me."

"Then show me how grateful."

"Please . . ."

Graves crossed to the bed in only a few steps. He slapped her once, hard, across the mouth.

"I said show me how grateful you are."

Then he started to take his clothes off. She watched him with a mixture of contempt and interest. What held her interest was the knife he wore inside his trousers. He lay this on the rickety wooden table next to the cot before he climbed into bed next to her.

"Now," he said, "why don't I help you out of your clothes, hmm?"

He had never seen a whore cry before, or tremble the way Jessica was.

He had to admit that he enjoyed the feeling it gave him—a feeling of power.

THIRTY-FOUR

When Clint reached the second floor of the parson's place he heard shouting from the opposite end of the hallway. A group of men ran to the top of the stairs and yelled down to the parson, who appeared a moment later. Clint found an unlocked door and slipped into an empty bedroom.

"What's wrong?" the parson called out.

"She's gone!"

"Gone? What do you mean she's gone?"

The other man spread his hands helplessly and said, "She's just gone."

"How did she get free of the ropes?"

The men just looked confused.

"Well, were they cut?" the Parson demanded.

"No."

"Have you searched the house?"

"Just up here."

Clint figured that he must have gotten to the first floor just after they finished their search.

"And there's no sign of her whatsoever?"

"None."

The parson began to pace.

"I can't believe this. She was naked, where could she have gone?"

"Her clothes are gone," one of the men offered.

"That's fine!"

The parson sounded in so much less control of himself than usual that Clint decided to make a move. He opened the door and stepped out into the hall, levelling the rifle at all the men.

"If anything happens to Jessica, Parson, I'm going to hold you personally responsible—and I'm not as nice as the Sheriff. I don't have to worry about any upcoming elections."

"How did you get up here?" the parson nearly screamed.

"The back way."

"Somebody left the back door open?" the parson demanded, looking at his men.

The men looked at each other and then at their feet. Obviously somebody had made a very big mistake.

"Just remember, Robeson," Clint said, "if anything's happened to her, I'm coming back for you."

Clint backed his way to the stairs and down, and went out the door.

"Gone?" Sheriff Halsey said when he met up with Clint Adams.

"Yes." Clint nodded to the surrounding houses and said, "I guess we'll have to ask around if anyone's seen anything in the past twenty minutes."

"These people are the parson's people," Halsey said. "You're not going to get any help out of them."

"Maybe somebody will talk," Clint said. "I'm willing to give it a try, otherwise I don't know where the hell she is—and remember, I'm not convinced that our killer has been caught."

"All right," Halsey said, "I'll help you, but did it ever occur to you that maybe she got away on her own?"

"Somehow, I don't think so."

They split up then, Clint taking the houses to the west and Halsey the ones to the east.

The first four houses gave Clint the same thing—a look of suspicion, and no help at all.

The next two residents were actually more cooperative, but they had nothing to offer.

At the seventh house, Clint's luck changed.

The owner, a potbellied little man in long john tops and sloppy pants held up by suspenders, said "Yep, I seen somebody."

"Who?"

"Two of 'em, actually."

"Two people?"

"Yep."

"Was one of them a woman?"

The man's eyes lit up and he said, "Sure was. One of them whores that works at Selena's—the real good looking one."

"Jessica?"

"That's her."

"And who was with her?"

"That little guy who always wears those ugly checkered suits."

"You mean the reporter, Graves?"

"Yep. That's right. Graves."

"Did you see where they were headed?"

"Couldn't tell, 'ceptin' they went south, in the direction of town."

"How long ago was this?"

"Oh, mebbe half an hour now, mebbe a little bit more."

"Tell me this. Did she look like she was going with him willingly?"

The man frowned and said, "Now that you mention it, he *was* walking behind her, and he did give her a little shove once in a while."

"All right, thank you. I appreciate your cooperation."

"He in trouble?"

"Who?"

"This Graves fella. Is he in trouble?"

"He could be, yes."

"Good. I seen him around and I never did like him."

"Me neither," Clint said, and left to find the sheriff.

When he caught up with Halsey the man was on the steps of a house, letting a doughy faced woman in a housedress tell him all the things she didn't like about Dante, in general, and his administration in particular.

"All I can say, ma'am, is that there's an election coming up and you can vote against me."

"Believe me, Sheriff," the woman said, her face flushed, "that's exactly what I intend to do."

On the street Clint said, "Looks like you've got yourself an admirer."

"That's the problem with elective offices," the sheriff said. "You have to listen to everybody who's got a complaint—and around Dante, that's damned near everybody."

"Why not try another town?"

The sheriff shrugged.

"Been here too long. I'm too old to start changing locations. What'd you find out?"

Clint told him what the man had seen, Graves and Jessica together.

"Where would he take her?" he asked the law-man.

"Hard to say," the sheriff said.

Clint nodded. As he started to hook his thumbs into his back pockets his fingers touched a large sheet of paper.

"Damn," he said, "I forgot all about this."

"What's that?"

"That photograph from the fire—the one the prostitute said had something to do with the Ripper."

"That's right," the lawman said. "I forgot about that, too."

"Let's head back to your office and have some coffee and figure this out."

"All right. Meanwhile, maybe I'll get an idea about where Graves would take Jessica."

THIRTY-FIVE

She had told him it would be better for both of them if they had something to drink first. Graves finally conceded the point. He got up, put his clothes on and went out front to the saloon to get some liquor.

He returned with two smudged glasses and a quart of rotgut whiskey. He carried it on a battered metal tray, as if this was a fancy establishment serving only the best in alcohol.

He placed it on the wooden table and poured them each a drink.

She still hadn't taken her clothes off. Her expression was inscrutable. Sometimes she seemed to be smiling for no reason at all. This made Graves nervous, very nervous.

He sat down on the cot to have his drink. He hadn't undressed this time.

"Where are you from?" he asked her.

She sipped her liquor, squinting from the sting of it.

"Nebraska."

"How did you ever get started in this business?"

She gave him a strange look.

"I had a sister."

He let a moment go by, waiting for more.

"You had a sister? I don't understand?"

"I had an older sister I admired very much, loved very much."

"Yeah—and so?"

"So some ladies talked her into doing things she wouldn't have done otherwise. We were very poor and my sister was looking for a way to help our family."

"That still doesn't explain how you got into this business," he said, confused.

The smile again, the odd one. The one that made him nervous. She was supposed to be here against her will but she wasn't acting like it.

"Maybe I'll tell you more later."

Then Graves noticed that she wasn't looking at him when she smiled, but at the knife on the table.

It was then he realized that she was probably afraid of him.

She thought he was the Ripper!

The sheriff did better than just coffee. He had a deputy run up the street and get them some sweet rolls, too.

Clint put the photograph on the Sheriff's desk and stared at it. It was the first time he'd really looked at it in a good light.

"I'll be damned."

"What?"

"Look at this."

He pushed the photograph over to the sheriff. A

third of the picture had been burned off in the fire but he was still able to see the group of five women.

"Look," he said, pointing. "This one is Marcie, the whore who was killed last night."

"There's a lot more here than just Marcie, Clint," the sheriff said. "The women in the picture are the women who have been killed by the Ripper."

"And look at this one," Clint said. "Do you know who this looks like?"

The sheriff looked more closely.

In the center of the women was one who looked very familiar. The sheriff frowned.

"Damn, I feel I know her."

"Well, you know somebody who looks a lot like her."

"Who?"

"Jessica."

"That's it!"

"This woman must be some relation to Jessica—a sister or something."

"I wonder where this photo was taken?"

Clint shrugged.

"I think we better get over to the hotel and ask Selena about this."

"What about the rolls?" the sheriff asked. "I was kind of looking forward to them."

Clint smiled.

"OK, let's take some along."

THIRTY-SIX

Graves was on the bed with Jessica, one leg hitched up on the mattress, the other on the floor. His moneybelt was under the bed.

His head was buzzing from the rye he'd been drinking. In his drunken state he realized that she had finally taken her clothes off, but that she was sitting with her back to him.

He leaned over to look at her and she was even more beautiful than ever.

If that was possible.

"Why don't you try some rye?" he asked her.

"I'm not much of a drinker, I'm afraid."

"It would do you good."

"Why don't you just have a little more?"

He poured himself some more and knocked it back quickly.

"You don't really want to get away from me, do you?" he asked her.

"It's nothing against you personally," she said. "I

just have to be alone sometimes."

"You mean, like now?"

She didn't answer.

"Now, Jessica?"

Still no reply.

"Well, believe me, now you can be alone and safe."

"Why?"

Her back remained to him. He ran his finger down her spine and the feel of her flesh made him tingle.

"Because I found the Ripper."

He felt her stir, heard her gasp. Triumphantly he thought, I've impressed her.

"You found the Ripper?"

"Yes, indeed."

Now she turned to look at him over her shoulder. Even in the half light he saw that her face looked even stranger than before.

"Who is he?"

"Was," Graves said. "Was, you mean. He killed himself after killing that whore, last night. It must have been the guilt."

"What are you talking about?"

"I'm not the Ripper, Jessica. I know you think I am, but I'm not. He killed a whore last night and then the guilt must have gotten to him. He poisoned himself."

"That's impossible," she said.

"No, it's not impossible, little lady. Not with cyanide." He smiled. "You can use cyanide and you're dead right away."

"Why did you find him?"

She had turned to face him now and was sitting with her legs crossed, Indian fashion. He couldn't keep from staring at her breasts.

"What do you mean, why?"

"I mean, isn't that the business of the law?"

"You forget, little lady, I'm a reporter, and a right smart one, too. Besides, I would've been a fool not to discover him myself."

"Why is that?"

"Because of the reward. Colonel Porter gave me a lot of money for finding him. Now this town can return to normal, thanks to me."

The way he bragged, Graves realized, sounded like he almost believed himself that he had found the Ripper instead of turning some dumb helpless rube into the killer for his own purposes.

"So you did it for the money?"

"Yes," he said, smiling. "Isn't that what you do your business for—money?"

She leaned towards him and said, "Maybe I'm ready for some of that rye, now."

"You are? That makes me happy, Jessica," he said, drunkenly. "That makes me very happy."

He poured her some rye.

He didn't notice that, as he went about fixing them each a drink, she silently slid his knife from the table onto the bed, beneath the pillow.

Now she smiled, too.

THIRTY-SEVEN

"My God," Selena said, sinking back down on the bed in her hotel room. "I know who this is—it's Jessica's sister."

"Where is she now, Selena?"

Selena shook her head sadly.

"Dead, I'm afraid."

"Dead?"

"Yes, one of her customers got out of hand one night—one of those men who like to inflict pain on women—and went a little too far. He strangled her. I guess it was right after that the women started getting the letters."

"What letters?"

"Letters blaming them—the four women the Ripper killed—for turning Amy, Jessica's older sister, into a prostitute."

"Did they?"

"Yes, I suppose they did," Selena said.

She drank gin from a large glass and then shook her head, again.

"What's wrong?" Clint asked.

"Well, I guess I always felt a little guilty myself about what the girls did."

"Tell us what happened."

"Amy wasn't quite right in the head. Hadn't been since birth, I guess. I mean, she was beautiful, as you can see from the picture, but she wasn't—well, quite right. She was very . . . innocent, simple. I'm not even sure she ever knew exactly what she was doing.

"She liked giving people pleasure, the way children do, you know? Very trusting. So the girls thought it would be a good idea to have her spend one night as a prostitute, they thought she'd enjoy it. Amy had wandered away from her home anyway, and the girls sort of took her in and took care of her. Well, anyway, it was really sort of a joke. I mean, them making her into a whore and all. She sat down in the parlor with the rest of them in that Omaha cathouse, and what do you know? Nearly every man who came in there chose her. So she just sort of . . . stayed on and started doing it for real. And then she got killed."

"What about the letters?" Clint asked.

Selena shuddered.

"Scary, they were. They started coming once a week and all written in red ink. Like blood. Said that all the women who corrupted Amy were going to die." She looked at the two men grimly. "And you know, that's exactly what happened."

Selena sounded as if she were going to start crying.

Clint stood up and handed her the photograph.

"Do you remember when this was taken?"

"About a month before Amy was killed, I think.

Right here." She knocked back some more gin, using it to fight the tears. "I remember that Amy sent it home."

"Home?"

"Yes. That's how she was. All she knew was that these women were her friends. She didn't realize that anyone else looking at this picture was looking at a bunch of prostitutes. All her parents would have to do was take one look at this picture and they'd know what she had become."

"So it was her parents who were sending the letters?"

"I don't know."

"What about Jessica?"

"What about her?"

"Did it ever occur to you that she might have sent those letters?"

"Well, no, it didn't. When Jessica showed up she came well recommended. She was already a whore when she got here."

"But you all knew she was Amy's sister?"

"She told us, yes. That was why we accepted her so readily. What are you trying to say, that Jessica is the killer? That she knew we'd accept her and then started killing us off?"

Clint stared at her, then looked at Halsey.

"What do you think, Sheriff?"

"I think the same thing you do."

"Right," Clint said. "Jessica is the Ripper."

"Oh, my God," gasped Selena.

"She must have cut herself last night when Marcie started screaming, to make it look good in case anyone saw her."

"That's what I'd say."

"So then . . . Graves never did find the Ripper, did he?"

"I said that all along."

"So he killed that poor boy and made it look like he was the Ripper."

"Right again."

"He must be crazy."

"We'd better find them," Clint said, "before one of them turns up dead."

Graves was drunk enough now that he let himself lie back on the cot with his eyes closed.

"I'm ready any time you are, sweet thing," he said, feeling his cock stiffen in anticipation.

He was finally going to have her, and she was going to come willingly.

He was thinking of two things—how good her flesh would taste and feel, and how beautiful California would be when he got there—especially since he'd have a whole lot of money.

He laughed to himself, a drunken laugh that was half spittle when it came up, and said again, "Ready any time you are."

And that was when she did it.

She leaned over him so that her breasts touched his chest. When her nipples scraped him he caught his breath. She reached beneath the pillow, drew out the knife and plunged it down into the center of his chest.

He was a sinner and had to die.

He struggled for a few moments, trying in vain to pull the knife from his chest, but her strength was greater than his. Where there had been spittle at the corners of his mouth there was now blood.

He looked up at her with shocked eyes, not understanding what was happening to him. Then he died and it didn't matter.

THIRTY-EIGHT

Parson Robeson addressed some dozen of his men in the church—and they were armed.

These were men the parson had "hired" to be part of his flock, to act like the rest of them—outraged family men and women. In reality, these men were hired guns, ready to do his bidding.

Robeson's political ambitions were in jeopardy now. If he allowed the whores to remain in town, he would never be elected mayor, and mayor was just the first step to bigger and better things.

"Gentlemen, it is time for you to come out of your disguises. Mr. Jordan, are your men ready?"

Jordan was Robeson's "foreman."

"We're ready, Mr. Robeson."

"Now, I want this whore, Jordan. The one they call Jessica. Even if you and your men have to take her away from the sheriff. Do you understand?"

"Hey," Jordan said, "as long as you're paying the bills, you get whatever you want . . . Parson."

175

Robeson put his hand on his wounded arm then and said, "And if any of you men think you can take the Gunsmith with a gun, feel free to try it. There's a bonus for taking him down."

The men exchanged glances. There wasn't any one of them who thought they could outshoot the Gunsmith, but if they joined forces they might have a chance.

"All right get out there, and bring me that whore —I've got the tar and feathers, and all I need now is her."

"Where is she?" Jordan asked.

"I don't know that, Jordan," Robeson said, exasperated. "If I did I would go and get her myself. Turn this town upside down if you have to, but find her!"

Colonel Porter sat in his den smoking a cigar, thinking about the money he'd paid Rupert Graves—and he worried about the real Ripper.

Porter was no fool. He knew very well that the dead man, Evars, had not been the Ripper, but if the townspeople and the miners thought he was, then they'd come back. If burying some poor soul as the Ripper would bring the town back to life, then the money he'd paid Graves was well spent.

But what would happen if the Ripper struck again? How would he explain that?

Clint and Sheriff Halsey decided to go back to the sheriff's office and organize a search party.

"What are we looking for, Sheriff?" one of his deputies asked.

"We're looking for the prostitute Jessica, or the reporter, Graves."

"What do we do when we find them?"

"Bring them here and put them in a cell. They're both to be placed under arrest."

"For what?"

"Murder?"

"Which one of them?"

"Both of them."

"They're both the killer?"

"They're both killers, let's put it that way. Now get out there and find them."

When the deputies left Clint said, "I hope one of us finds Jessica and not one of them. She'll wrap them around her little finger."

"Do you think she really knows what she's doing, or is she sick?"

"That's not going to be for us to decide, Sheriff. A court of law will decide whether or not she's . . . totally sane. First, though, we've got to find her."

"Well, let's go."

As they left the sheriff's office Clint asked, "Where does Graves do most of his drinking?"

"The other side of town, I guess," Halsey said. "That is, when he couldn't afford better, but now he's got the Colonel's money he can drink wherever he wants."

"If he doesn't want to be found, however, he'll be on the other side of town. Let's start there."

"Right."

Jordan and his men split into pairs and began looking for Jessica. They went to the hotels and saloons, and during the course of their search their paths crossed those of Halsey's deputies.

Inevitably, their paths also crossed those of Clint's and the sheriff's, as well.

They had just asked the bartender in a place called the Camp Saloon if he had seen the whore, Jessica. He told them that they had just missed two men who were also looking for her.

"What'd they look like?" the sheriff asked.

"Well now, that's the funny thing, Sheriff. I could have sworn these two men were part of the parson's flock, but when they were in here they were wearing guns, and they looked like they knew how to use them."

"And they wanted Jessica?"

"That's right?"

"Did they ask about Graves, the little reporter with the checkered suits?"

"No, just the whore."

Clint looked at the sheriff and said, "Are you thinking what I'm thinking?"

"What?"

"I think the parson may finally be showing us his true colors."

"You mean, he's hired gunmen?"

"As a last resort—and this is it."

"If that's the case we'd better find Jessica first."

The sheriff turned back to the bartender and asked, "Have you seen Graves here tonight?"

"He was in here, yeah. He wanted to know if I had a back room to rent him, which I don't."

"Do you know somebody who might?"

"There's a few places," the bartender said, and listed three places, two of which they had already checked.

"This last one has to be it," Clint said. "Let's go."

THIRTY-NINE

As soon as they entered the saloon they knew immediately that it was the right place, because the bartender became very nervous.

"Where are they?" the sheriff asked.

"Sheriff, I don't know nothing—"

Clint reached over the bar and grabbed the man by the shirt front.

"Where?"

"Back room. They've been there for hours."

"Graves and the woman?"

"Yes."

Clint let him go and followed the sheriff to the back, where a doorway led to a hallway.

They stood outside the doorway, one on each side, and knocked.

"Graves?" Clint called.

No reply.

"Graves?" he called again, banging on the door.

Still nothing.

"We're going to have to go in," he said to Halsey.

"Be my guest."

Clint raised his foot and then slammed his heel into the door right above the doorknob. The wood splintered and the door slammed open and then fell off its hinges.

He went into the room with the Sheriff right behind him. The smell got to them immediately. There is nothing quite like the stench of death, and the room was filled with it. Graves was sprawled on the bed, the handle of a knife sticking up out of his chest. It was plain from the amount of blood all over the room that he was dead. He'd probably been dead for quite a while.

Jessica sat in a straightbacked wooden chair, staring at the bed, at her handiwork.

"Jessica," Clint said.

She looked up at him.

"They shouldn't have done what they did to her, you know," she said.

"I know, Jessica."

"They corrupted her."

"Yes."

"And then that man killed her. That was their fault, too. If they hadn't made her into a whore she never would have been killed. She'd be alive today."

"I suppose that's true, Jessica, but—"

She looked at the sheriff and said, "I killed them all, you know."

"We know," he said.

"And I killed him," she said, gesturing to Graves' body on the bed. "He deserved to be killed. He killed an innocent man and made it look like he was the Ripper."

"We know that, too, Jessica. We know it all. We're here to help you."

"I never called myself the Ripper, you know."

"That was him," the sheriff said. "When he got here all he talked about was the Ripper."

"I just wanted to make them pay."

"And you did," Clint said.

"I suppose I'll be hanged."

"It's a possibility," Halsey said.

"I don't mind. I'm not afraid. I'll be with Amy, then."

"Jessica, come on, come with us—" Clint started to say.

"It's the truth, you know," she said, looking up at them both. "I'm not afraid to hang."

She looked at Clint now and said, "Do you blame me for what I did, Clint?"

"I don't think it was right, Jessica. I'm sorry."

"That's all right. You're a good man."

She started crying then, and he went to her and helped her to her feet.

"How is your arm?"

"It's all right. I knew just how badly to injure myself. It's all right."

"Let's go, then. We'll have the doctor look at it, anyway."

"I talk to her every morning, you know."

"To—"

"Amy. She talks to me. She's the one who told me to kill them. I wanted to make her happy."

Clint and Halsey exchanged glances. There was no longer any doubt in their minds about Jessica's sanity.

As they stepped out of the saloon Clint became aware of the four men across the street. The men had seen them, too.

"Sheriff," he said.

Halsey looked up just as the men started to walk across.

"Sheriff," one of them said.

"Can I help you?"

"My name's Jordan. I work for the Parson."

"Good for you."

"He'd like to see this . . . lady right away."

"The lady is going with me. Tell the parson it's all over. She is under arrest for murder."

The sheriff took her elbow in his hand, while Clint took the other, and they started forward only to have their path blocked by the four men.

"I'm sorry, Sheriff," Jordan said, "but the Parson is paying me to bring her to him."

"Is he paying you enough to die?" Clint asked.

Jordan looked at him and said, "So you're the Gunsmith, huh?"

"That's right."

"There's four of us, Gunsmith, and we're pros."

"Then you should know when to back off. A pro always does."

"I never back off."

"Then if you try to take this girl away from me, you're a dead man."

Jordan and Clint and exchanged hard stares.

"I've got to try," Jordan said, and went for his gun.

Clint pushed Jessica behind him immediately and drew, firing into the man's chest. He was aware of Halsey's gun going off next to him. The other men went for their guns. He fired at another man, catching him in the stomach, and shot a third man in the chest. By this time the sheriff had shot the fourth man, who was falling to the ground. The man squeezed the trigger of his gun reflexively as he fell, firing one shot that went wild.

"You all right?" Clint asked the Sheriff.

"Yeah, you?"

"Fine."

They both turned to look for Jessica and saw her lying on the boardwalk, her chest bloody. She was already dead, without even any time for last words.

FORTY

Clint spent the night alone in the hotel. At dawn he got up and went to the livery where Duke and the rig waited for him.

When he came out into the overcast morning, Sheriff Halsey was waiting.

"You're an early riser," the lawman said.

"I could say the same for you."

Halsey's eyes bore into Clint's.

"She got to you, didn't she?"

"I'd have to say yes, she did. Did you return the colonel's money?"

"I did. He was pretty satisfied that the real killer was caught. He can go back to building up his mine now."

"I guess I'm glad for him. What about the Parson? What's happening with him?"

"I had my men talk to his men this morning, and I talked to a lot of members of his flock. I think the parson's going to be moving on."

"The only thing we have in common."

"You could stick around for a while, you know?"

"No," Clint said, looking at the sky. "It's time to move on."

"For some of us," Halsey said. "We just do the best we can, I guess."

Thinking of Jessica and the prostitutes, of the parson and the colonel, he said, "That's what we do, all right."

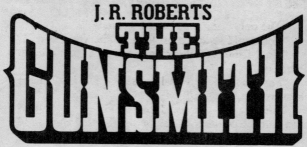

J. R. ROBERTS
THE GUNSMITH

SERIES

Available at your local bookstore or return this form to

 CHARTER
THE BERKLEY PUBLISHING GROUP, Dept. B
390 Murray Hill Parkway, East Rutherford, NJ 07073

Please send me the titles checked above. I enclose _____ Include $1.00 for postage
and handling if one book is ordered: add 25¢ per book for two or more not to exceed
$1.75 CA, IL, NJ, NY, PA, and TN residents please add sales tax. Prices subject to change
without notice and may be higher in Canada

NAME _____

ADDRESS _____

CITY _____ STATE/ZIP _____

(Allow six weeks for delivery.)